RACHEL ANNE JONES

 **Days**
as
an
ATM

ISBN: 979-8-88653-399-6

Published by Satin Romance
An Imprint of Melange Books, LLC
White Bear Lake, MN 55110
www.satinromance.com

Published in the United States of America.

Cover Design by Ashley Redbird Designs

For Douglas—always.

For my children Isaac, Isabel, and Abby, thanks for loving me and my weird mind.

For my friends, family, and readers, thank you for your continued support.

To Nancy, thanks for believing in my story.

To Caroline and Ashley, thanks for the amazing book covers.

1

DAY ONE

Badge 343

ou're living on the wrong side of paradise," Preacher says as he pops his head out the door.

"Maybe so, but there's somethin' to be said for consistency," I reply while resisting the urge to exert my position of authority as the sheriff over a man of God.

"You gonna hang out on my steps all day?"

"Yep."

"You know you're the only one who lingers," he muses. "Kinda makes a person wonder."

Preacher just said one word too many. I look up at him from beneath the wide brim of my hat. "It's not Sunday. I'm sittin' outside. This is a public place and my designated thinkin' spot, so if you don't mind leavin' me to my silence, I'd 'preciate it."

He looks me over long enough to tell me I'm the fool I know I'm bein'. "It's interesting how much you like some rules," he looks back at the cross above the church doors, "but others you could care less about."

"I'm committed to my job, Preacher. You know that."

He sniffs. "Well, Sheriff. At least you're committed to something." My shoulders tense. The muscles in my legs twitch. I'm two seconds away from springin' up like a jack-in-the box. If he were any other man in this town, I'd have him by the shirt collar. I know that and he knows that which must be why his hands are in the air, and I didn't even pull my gun.

"I'm just saying."

"What? What are you sayin'?" I ask, but I don't know why. We've only had this conversation about half a dozen times.

"You're a nice enough guy. You do a good job. I like you just fine, Sheriff, but I'd like you a whole lot better if you were sitting in a pew."

"That makes one of us," I bark.

"I gotta do my job just like you do yours," he mutters before shakin' his head and walkin' back inside, closin' the door quietly behind him.

I stare at the church door a little too hard and a little too long. Preacher interrupted my thinkin' process and ruined the rest of my mornin'. I take a sip of mostly cold coffee that's probably gonna have me in the nearest bathroom in about four minutes. My concentration is shot, and if I'm not mistaken a few nosy old ladies are starin' out their windows at me from across the street. It was good business sense buildin' this church across from the old folk's home. Makes it easier for Preacher to nab them on their way out.

I cross the street to toss my coffee in the trashcan. Bennie steps outside in her scrubs and gives me a friendly wave. Her scrubs are a little snug. I wish I didn't know she doesn't mind my noticin'.

"Hey, Sheriff."

"Bennie," I say before spinnin' around and headin' for the sidewalk.

Preacher's words ramble around inside my head. The thing about arguin' with a man of God, even if you get the last word, it doesn't feel like you're winnin'. And I hate to lose. I hate it more than I love to win.

My mind returns to what I was workin' on before Preacher started hecklin' me. I've got the cell phone of a missin' girl who's in a whole lotta trouble, and that was before she went missin'. The problem is, I made a promise, and if there's anythin' redeemable about me, it's that I'm a man of my word. I made a vow to her mother I'd watch out for her. I don't intend to break it.

2

CRACK-IT

This pact is made between twelve-year-old Susan Tripp and twelve-year-old Meagan Davis on the third day of August in the year of the honeybee. The rules of the game are top secret. If Meagan or Susan tells anyone these rules, may they fall down a well filled with fire ants and die.

1. Take no prisoners.
2. Play to win.
3. There are no boundaries.
4. Once the mystery is solved, the game starts over.
5. There are two players–Meagan and Susan.
6. No other players allowed.
7. If you bring other players into Crack-It, you lose.
8. If you lose, you cannot start the next Crack-It challenge.
9. If you don't start the game, you must solve the mystery.
10. If you solve the mystery, you have won at Crack-It.
11. If you win at Crack-It, you own the next mystery.
12. If the mystery beats you, you've Cracked.
13. There is no such thing as luck. There is only skill, vigilance, and consequence. Let the games begin.

3

SNACK TIME - SALT & VINEGAR

he thing about a chip is, it's not a crack, and if you chip a little away at a time here and there, it can be a carefully constructed dance that pings at the foundation but leaves it intact. I'd like to think I'm a master at chipping.

"Susan," my kind-hearted therapist says in her Zen tone that is manipulative in itself. Kerin speaks in such a manner that I often forget she is the enemy, a fact I forgive each time I remember, because I understand it all too well. She is who she is, and she cannot help herself. Although it is her duty to help me work on me, it is also her job to interrogate me without appearing as if she is digging. I am the dirt that holds fragments of truth which I release as slowly and painfully as the manner Meagan Davis tried to destroy me. I'm not ready to give up. Chipping changes the shape of something but if it's done right, it won't break it.

A crack is irreparable. I hope I've got a ways to go before I'm broken.

"Yes," I answer.

"Where did we leave off?"

I resist the urge to roll my brown eyes that Meagan told me are the color of shit the first day I met her, and even though I know now she was just saying that to get a reaction because that's what she does, I never could get that thought out of my head. Mom always said Meagan was a little too clairvoyant for her own good.

5

I always thought Mom just liked the word clairvoyant because it's in her favorite movie, *Big Stone Gap*. And then Dad would respond to Mom's off the wall comment about Meagan, telling us that we're both nuts, and no one can predict the future, especially not a pissed off teenage girl who says things just to say them, which is probably what I'm about to do while lying on a loveseat feeling nothing like a sweetheart. It's probably not the best idea to lie to Kerin when my parents are paying her serious money for me to tell the truth, but I never asked to go to therapy.

I stare up at the ceiling as I lay with one leg half-sprawled over the back of Kerin's faded green and white plaid loveseat while the other stretches out straight. "Why don't you get new furniture?" I ask. "I'm sure you can afford it," I say, because I really want to know, but also, I'm deflecting, as Mom would say if she were here. Mom has added to her already extensive vocabulary since I started therapy three months ago, much to my father's chagrin.

I'd rather talk about surface stuff–how lately Mom's favorite nickname for my dad is *insensitive a-hole* and his term of endearment for her is *Joan of Arc*. I could go on for hours about the fact that I've slowly morphed from a girl to a ghost since Meagan Davis set foot in my home. She's a human wrecking ball, but she's also my best friend. I guess that makes me the wreckage. "Where did we leave off?" I repeat Kerin's question while searching my mind for what information I want her to know. My mind is a total blank.

"You were worried about the upcoming dance."

I resist the urge to giggle. My worries about the upcoming dance seem so unimportant. All I can think of is the dark promise *he* made to me as we stood on the bridge that night. I shook from head to toe with fear. I was so terrified I didn't know how I was still standing. I didn't have to look at him to know he stood as still as death, clutching the gun he pointed at me, making me wonder if I was next.

"You've done it now, girl. Remember that. You are part of it. If I go down, you'll go down with me."

I was so confused. I'd done everything he told me to do. All I could do was stare at the night sky. I didn't dare look over the bridge into the waters below to see where the current took her, my best friend. It was so cold. My hands were numb. I think. Or maybe I just didn't want to feel any part of me that was capable of literally throwing away the last piece of my bumpy friendship with Meagan Davis.

"I did what you told me to," I said, because I couldn't say nothing else, and because it was the truth. "You said if I did that, you would leave me alone."

He laughed. I almost peed myself. I didn't think he could get any scarier than he already was. "Susan."

I didn't know he knew my name.

"You did that so *you'll* leave me alone," he explained to me as if I was a toddler, or someone so simple I could not comprehend what I had just done. "If you *even* think about talking, just remember, you are an accessory to murder."

Before I could say any more, I heard his footsteps. I didn't turn to look. I couldn't. I didn't want to see anything about him.

"You would do well to forget her. Forget everything you ever knew about Meagan. She was never here."

Tears rolled down my cheeks. All I wanted to do was forget I was ever there. A car door shut. His headlights lit up the side of my face before they faded, just like the sound of his engine. I don't know how long I stood there staring into nothing. His words followed me into my car and all the way home. They whispered in my ears when I tried to sleep. *Accessory to murder*. Me. A fifteen-year-old girl.

I never thought I'd be capable of such a thing. I have judged myself a thousand times since that night. I've examined my actions from every angle. I have tried to think of any other way it could have gone, and I have come to this conclusion, I will do whatever it takes to protect my parents. Maybe that makes me stupid, just like the man said, but I have no choice. They know nothing about the man, or the childhood game Meagan started way back when. They are innocent. I am not. I threw her in the river. Whatever comes down on me has nothing to do with them. "The dance, right," I say as I weave my fingers together on my stomach which grows tighter and smaller by the second. I can

7

hardly eat. "Well, I just started sort of talking to Ryan, the football player, but he hasn't asked me to the dance yet," I answer, and then I say no more because my throat tightens, and my eyes water. It's so dumb that in the middle of all this, I'm still crying over a guy who never should have dated me in the first place. He's popular, hot, and charming. I'm the quiet, weird girl who can be tricked into playing some strange, twisted game that ends with murder. All this time, I could have walked away, but I didn't.

"Maybe he's waiting to do a Promposal," Kerin says with a kind smile.

"This isn't prom," I argue, even though I know I'm being difficult.

"Well, you know what I'm saying," she says in a teasing voice, but it's not mean.

"He's not going to," I say as my hands break free from each other. I fiddle with a stray string on the bottom of my shirt.

"I wouldn't give up on him yet," she coaxes.

I can't answer. If I do, I might cry. Ryan won't be asking me anything or sending me any more flirty little texts. He told me we're taking a beat because we got too serious.

I didn't answer him then, just like I'm not answering Kerin now. I knew he was lying but I wasn't ready for the truth. I'm a criminal, an outcast. I may as well be a school shooter. Of course, Ryan wants nothing to do with me.

She clears her throat. I sneak a frequent glance in her direction and muster up the courage to mirror her reassuring smile. "Yeah. Maybe he will," I agree while choking on kindness I do not deserve.

4

Badge 343

n the past five years I've had some experiences I'd like to forget. I've busted down a door or two for domestic violence cases, chased some meth-head runners through the woods, and witnessed the aftermath of a few horrific car wrecks. Those moments filled with me fear and adrenaline all at the same time, but not a one of 'em shook me clean down to my toes.

Revisitin' the scene of the one who got away has me so tied up I'm seconds away from grippin' the porch railin' and spewin' crackers. My hand shoots out from my side and pounds on the door to the part of my past I can't let go. Marlena O'Reilly.

"Hold yer horses, son. I'm comin'," a tired voice calls from behind the screen door.

A wrinkled hand appears on the doorframe. She stands in the shadows. "Hello there, tall, dark and handsome," she states. It's a compliment loaded with resentment, and it leaves me feeling bared in more ways than one. "No flowers this time?"

One thing about O'Reilly women, they drill you with truths you'd love to forget. "Ms. O'Reilly," I answer. "May I come in?"

The floor creaks. Her shadow disappears. "You gonna come in, or ain't ya?"

I tug the door open. The room lights are dim, but I still see the bookshelves which cover every wall. I can't help but smile. I remember bein' surprised at all the books the last time I was here. Twelve years ago.

"You're the first person I've seen on this road in about four years," she says as she shuffles into the kitchen, opens the fridge, and pours lemonade into two mason jars before settin' them on the small, square table. Everythin' looks exactly the same, includin' the dated refrigerator magnet missin' a fourth of the corner featurin' a glamorous woman trapped by her own beauty. I find myself starin' at it like I did all those years ago, just as captivated. But there's another magnet beside it. It looks new. I step closer and squint to read the quote. "I used to be Snow White, but I drifted. –Mae West"

It's just a magnet, but I can't help but wonder if it was Marlena or Meagan who gave it to this woman standin' here in her kitchen starin' me down with courage and nerve. If I didn't know better, I'd say she wears a holster, and not me.

I wonder if Ms. O'Reilly will deliver the same news this time. I wonder if she'll tell me again with a smirk on her face, a light in her eyes, and no pity in her voice for me, just another guy lookin' to show her wayward daughter a good time, that I don't have what it takes to catch an O'Reilly woman's attention.

"I appreciate you lettin' me meet my granddaughter." Her words hit me like bullets, but her eyes are watery. I look away out of respect. I know how hard that was for her to say.

I clear my throat. "I didn't take that call."

"I knew it was you who allowed it. You were always kind to us. That's not somethin' a woman like me forgets."

Her eyes roam over me, takin' their time. I made it through the academy. I've had officers scream in my face. I've been jumped by a prisoner in the yard. Nothin' makes me feel as transparent and terrified as this grey-haired woman lookin' at me like a grizzly bear eyes their next dinner. Her gaze stops on my hand. "You're not married."

I resist the urge to cover one hand with the other. "Divorced."

"Children?"

My heart pinches when I remember Sam's two boys. I hope they're doin' alright. "None of my own."

She studies me some more. "She step out on you?"

I hate her question. No matter how many times I've been told there's nothin' I could've done, knowin' my wife left me for another man makes me feel lacking. "What makes you say that?" I ask, even though I know I'm takin' the bait.

"I know men. You're not the cheatin' kind."

I don't know if that makes me feel worse or better. "Thanks." I manage.

"Who was he?"

I've already said more than I wanted to, but I've been told O'Reilly women have a way of makin' men spill their secrets. It just doesn't usually happen at the kitchen table.

"No one you know," I answer in an authoritative tone that leaves a lot of guys shakin' in their boots.

Her hand smacks the table, makin' me jump. "I suppose." The table slides just enough to spill some salt. She wipes the surface clean. The tabletop is white, save for a patch of brown here and there. I wish I wasn't so observant. "I did the best I could. I did what I thought was right. I loved her as much as I was able."

She looks me in the eye. "What are you here for?"

Her words fill my ears like a slow tide that just keeps on risin', not carin' who it drowns. Her question hits me between the eyes, along with the fact she's been interrogatin' me, not the other way around. "We might have a missin' girl on our hands."

She laughs at me, adding insult to injury. I can tell from the gleam in her eye she knows I know she slighted me. "You don't know if she's gone missing? Isn't that your job?"

As hard as it is, I hold her stare. Feeling inept in this woman's presence is nothin' new for me. "She may have run away. We just don't know."

Silence falls between us. Seconds drag by. "And you think I know somethin' about all this." She blinks. Her eyes widen. A sense of awareness enters the room. "It's Meagan."

I nod my head. "Have you heard from her?"

Her lips form a flat line. "No."

"Will you tell me if you do?"

Huggin' herself, she looks off to the side. "Maybe."

It's not the response I wanted, but her answer doesn't surprise me. "It's our job to keep her safe."

"She might have enough O'Reilly in her to keep her one step ahead," she murmurs. "We'll see."

It might make me a fool, but I have to ask. "Mind if I take a look around?"

Her jaw twitches just a hair, but I catch it. "You gotta piece of paper from the judge?" she challenges.

"No."

Her eyes light up. A slow smile spreads. For a second or two, the years fade. "You didn't sneak in my daughter's bedroom back then, and you're not gettin' in it now."

My mouth goes dry, but somehow, I keep it closed. My few moments of grace with Ms. O'Reilly just ran out. "All I did was ask her to the dance," I protest.

She nods. "I remember." She gives me a wink. "You came to the front door. That was your first mistake. If you really knew her, you would've come to her window."

Her hardened tone is almost too much to take. A feeling of emptiness chills me to the bone. I wonder if the worn woman in front of me had a day in her life when someone didn't demand something she wasn't willin' to give. And now here I am, pokin' around in an unwanted past she didn't create, but it's shared history between us.

Ms. O'Reilly is a haunted woman. I wonder how long her only daughter will haunt me.

"How did you know I never…" I stop talkin'. Her eyebrow raises. She's gonna make me say it if I want an answer. "I mean that we never…" I drop my hands on the table. Like many other questions I have about Marlena, this one will also go unanswered.

She leans back in her chair. Her two empty fingers steady as if she's holdin' a cigarette. She eyes the empty ashtray. "A mother knows," she murmurs more to herself than me. "A mother always knows."

I had other thoughts, but my mind draws a blank as I look around as much as I dare. "Well, I 'spect that's my cue to leave." I say a little too loud.

"You didn't touch your lemonade," she scolds in a not-so-gentle tone, a tell-tale sign her tired eyes aren't as negligent as the CPS neglect or abuse report my mother wrote suggested all those years ago.

I pick up the glass I haven't touched since she set it on the table. I down the lukewarm lemonade.

It seems Ms. O'Reilly is slippin'. She's not as hard as she appears. She musta seen my car comin' from a mile away. If I didn't know better, I'd say she made the lemonade just for me. "What was my second mistake?" I ask, once I'm on my feet.

She blinks once more. Her eyes remain on high alert. "Bein' who you are."

"And who's that?" I ask, expectin' yet another comment from a possessive grandmother about the law interferin' where it doesn't belong when it comes to her daughter and granddaughter.

"A protector with gentle hands. Your heart is too pure for an O'Reilly woman. That's just the way things is." She makes a strange noise with her teeth. "We know who we are. We've accepted it. You need to too. Stop lookin' for that girl. She'll turn up soon or she won't. Either way she'll get through it, and she won't take your help."

I back away from her, knowin' it makes me look weak, but I can't help it. The woman gives me the willies. "I'm just doin' my job, Mims. You know that."

She flashes me a smile, barin' her front teeth. "And I'm doin' mine."

I'm halfway across the room when a picture snags my attention. Long black hair hangs free, a freckle or two on that turned-up nose, and green eyes which look like emeralds stare back at me through the dusty glass. It has me mesmerized. I'm right back in high-school and struck down once more by the beauty that is

Marlena O'Reilly, a girl as wild and crazy as her last name implies. Her eyes shine bright with a natural curiosity.

"I should have known my past would catch up to me," Ms. O'Reilly says with one foot in the kitchen and the other in the dinin' room. Her cryptic statement wreaks havoc with my inquisitive nature, but I keep my mouth shut. Her need for control is as obvious as a flashin' neon sign. "Once that girl learnt how she came about, no amount of boys or men could satisfy her want for revenge on any guy she met. I didn't know PTSD was hereditary," she jokes, but it falls flat.

I feel terrible. The last thing an O'Reilly wants is pity.

"It was an accident. I didn't mean for her to find out." Her words are heavy with regret.

I have no reason to doubt them.

"I should have known there was no keepin' secrets from Marlena."

The way her voice cracks on her daughter's name splits me in two. I find myself wishin', like so many times before, that they could have had a different life. I can't help but wonder had they not lived in the same house for three generations, surrounded by the sins of their absent fathers, could the O'Reilly women have learned love and pain should be two separate emotions.

5

DAY TWO

om and I sit at the table in a small room. I glance in her direction from the corner of my eye. She stares straight ahead, as if she's imagining she's anywhere else but here. I wish I could do the same. Whatever happens, I will not fall apart. If I do, Meagan wins.

Mom squeezes my hand one time. It's the first time she's touched me since we left the house to drive to the police station. Past conversations burn my ears and roll through my brain like Dad's socked feet that paced the kitchen floor in silence. "This is what we get for taking her in. This is what we get for trying to do something good," he hissed at Mom and I as the three of us hovered in our separate corners.

"Stop it, Jeff. We can't think about any of that now. We need to focus on saving our daughter," Mom begged.

"That's why we need a lawyer, Nell." The words fell out of his mouth all bumpy and weird, like chipped marbles that don't roll. I hate it when they call each other by their first names. It means they're angrier than they should be for being married to each other.

"We can't afford it, Jeff. You know this. It's not in our budget," she said, and I braced myself. Budget may as well be another curse word in our house, along with the word "No," both of which my mother is an expert at saying, except to her brother, who inevitably enters every conversation in the span of about five seconds that turns into a "discussion" between my parents.

"Why don't you ask *your brother* to pay for an attorney?" My father spat. "You ask him for everything else."

"He hired you, Jeff. Don't forget that," Mom warned.

"Yeah, yeah. I know. He hired me, a worthless, washed-up, middle-aged man with a failing restaurant who bankrupted his family in five years' time. You don't have to throw it in my face, Nell. Your brother *saved us*. We should all be eternally grateful to him," my father grumbled like he does when he's feeling angry and frustrated.

I stood there, an unwilling audience to their marital problems being splattered all over Mom's kitchen walls like their own personal rebellion against her habitual OCD. Mom took cleaning to a whole new level even before the virus came along. Meagan always joked the virus did us all a favor by making my mother not look as crazy as she really is. I gave Meagan a glare when she said it out of loyalty to Mom, even though I mostly agreed with her. Meagan stared me down with an unapologetic look on her face. "Who else do you know who literally wipes down canned goods with bleach water before putting them in a cupboard that's dusted once a week?" Meagan demanded, at which time I ducked my head. I was so embarrassed. I notice my mother's idiosyncrasies. I had hoped Meagan wouldn't.

These thoughts plagued me as I stared at the clock as hard as I could, wishing one of my parents would stop glaring at the other and look up. Other thoughts race through my mind too, like betraying my friendship with Meagan. Mom might have her uncontrollable habits, but at least there's a diagnosis tied to an explanation. What Meagan and I did together—there's no amount of logic or reasoning that would make any of it okay.

"I didn't say any of that, Jeff, and I never have," Mom answered in a soft voice, cutting into the beginning of my worst nightmare. "You berate yourself often enough. I don't need to." She snatched her purse off the counter. "I'm taking our daughter downtown to speak to the police. She's going to tell the truth. She's done nothing wrong. We'll get this sorted out. We'll be home before lunch." She sniffled but held her head high. "We don't need a lawyer to guard her words. All she has to do is tell the truth," she said again in a firm voice, a voice meant for me.

My head swam as I walked out of the house. When I was a kid, Meagan and I played a game. We would make up a mystery and leave clues for the other to solve. Meagan would always win. I was never good at making things up, nor was I good at wading through half-truths and sniffing out deception. Meagan may not be here in person, but she's still playing the game. And I am still losing. I don't know what the truth is anymore. So how can I tell it?

"Susan," I looked up at the sound of my name. Mom stood by our minivan, but I stood frozen in the middle of my sidewalk. "What are you doing? Get in the car."

I took a step forward and then another. We rode in silence to the police station. Disappointment rolled off Mom in waves, drowning me. I turned to look out the window and closed my eyes. I wished for the impossible. I wished I could go back to the time before, before what though? That was the question. My thoughts jumbled inside my head. I know Meagan and I had some good times together, many good times. But at that moment all I could think of were the bad ones. For a split second, I found myself agreeing with my dad. I wished I had never met Meagan. And then I just felt awful.

With every turn Mom made I bumped a little harder against the window. It felt like a sledgehammer knocking down my invisible dam. At the corner of Third and Carney, it became one hit too many and I broke. A horrible sound shot out of my mouth. Suddenly there weren't enough tears to cover what I'd done. I leaned over as snot flowed out of me, making me cough. A white waving Kleenex appeared in my lap. "For heaven's sake, Susan," Mom scolded. "Get a hold of yourself."

Relieved of having something to do, I took the Kleenex and started mopping up my mess. "You can't go in there looking like that," Mom said in her condescending tone, one that held no pity for me, her only child who can't seem to stay out of trouble.

My head popped up. I stared at her through my tears. "Like what, Mom? Like someone who just lost their best friend?"

Mom blinked. Pain flickered in her eyes, but as usual, I didn't know if it was because I yelled at her or if she had found an ounce of compassion in her heart of stone for my best friend, the one whom she never liked but tried to help just the same. I felt immediate remorse for yelling at her. It wasn't her fault. How could she know her good intentions with reaching out to Meagan would end up like this? How could she know four years later we'd lose Meagan anyway?

Mom swallowed hard. "I know, honey. I know you're hurting. We must be strong now. For Meagan."

I heard her words, and they made sense. I believed she meant them. But at the same time, they sounded scripted. I wiggled in my seat, despising myself. I don't know why I'm so critical of everyone all the time, or why I can't shut it off. I opened my mouth to answer. I didn't know how to tell her what she didn't know. Thoughts of the nameless, faceless voice filled me. "Whatever happens, you cannot tell. If you tell, you will follow your friend sooner than later," he'd said with a laugh that made as much sense as Meagan's motionless body sitting beside me in my car that night.

I flinch even now when I recall the ugly words I hurled at Meagan, words she couldn't hear because she was already gone. I was just so angry. Ever since I started dating Ryan, Meagan had become needier than ever. She had always been a little clingy, and I'd mostly understood. I couldn't imagine losing my parents so young, at any age really. We had just become best friends when she lost her mother, the only parent she knew. Meagan was a quiet girl. Her long, straight hair was as dark as her heart-shaped face was pale. She had bright green eyes that pierced you when you looked into them. Her freckles always struck me as being out of place. They suggested an accidental innocence I'm not sure she ever possessed. Even with all her intensity, I was her lifeline, and she was mine.

"Hello, Susan," the detective says. I sit up straighter in my chair. My hand automatically reaches for my mother, but it finds an empty chair. "I'm Detective Shallitt," he continues. My mind is somewhere else. Even though I know Meagan is gone, it feels like she's sitting right beside me.

"Did you know a shallot is not an onion? It's just an imitation. An onion has sharp taste. A shallot is sweeter. It cooks better." Meagan said to me in her all-knowing way. She gave me a playful nudge. "It's like us. I'm the onion. You're the shallot," she said with a giggle.

"Why can't we just be who we are?" I asked in a tired voice. I was so tired of her need to compare the two of us all the time, or her constant need to point out she was some sort of villain. I never saw her as a dangerous person. Maybe that's the problem.

"Hello," I manage as I look into the detective's hazel eyes that appear to be seeking the truth, but I know better. I've watched enough cop shows. This is a game. He's trying to get me to incriminate myself.

He taps his fingers on the table. "How well do you know Meagan Davis?"

I shift in my seat. "As well as you can know an onion," I answer.

He leans back in his seat and stares at me long enough to make me regret my words, but they're the truth. "What does that mean?"

I exhale slowly. "It means what I said. Onions have layers. Meagan had them. I knew what she wanted me to know," I reply. My voice breaks on the last word. Mom told me to speak the truth, and I am. I just didn't know how much it would hurt to say it out loud.

I wish I didn't notice Detective Shallitt kind of looks like Ryan Reynolds with his dark hair, intense stare, almost smirky face, and deliberate manner of speaking. "And what is it she wanted you to know?" he asks. It's the last question I expected.

"I don't know," I say. I can tell by the look on his face he thinks I'm lying. I've seen the same expression enough times on my father's face, and he wasn't wrong. Every one of those times Meagan was right there beside me. I'm not blaming Meagan for my lies, well, not exactly. All I know is she had a way of talking me into doing things I would not do alone. Things that usually had some element of danger attached to them. There are different types of danger. There's the kind that gets you a sprained ankle, or a bloody nose, or grounded for a week. And then there's the kind that has you sitting at a table lying to a cop while trying to look innocent when you know you are anything but.

"You just said you knew what she wanted you to know, and now you're saying you don't know what that is," Detective Shallitt states, and his argument is valid. It makes perfect sense. The trouble is, so does mine.

I nod my head. "Exactly. She didn't want me to know anything," I protest. "Or at least not anything real. Everything was a game to her."

We sit here with a table between us, but it might as well be a bottomless pit. He wants answers that I can't give because I don't know them. If I did know them, I might not be alive. Whatever Meagan knew is what got her killed. The revelation catches me by surprise all over again. Someone killed my best friend. It was probably the man in the car. The one who made sure I'd keep my mouth shut by uttering three little words that haunt me day and night—*accessory to murder,* or as Meagan would say if she were here, ATM. She had a thing for acronyms. She also had a thing for creating her own definition of the truth.

"Do you know why you are here?" Detective Shallitt asks in a softer voice, as if that's going to cause a bunch of words to come flying out of my mouth.

"No," I say, because I have an idea why I'm there, but I'm not one hundred percent sure.

"You're here because you are the last person who was seen with Meagan Davis when she was still alive," he says in a calm voice I wish I could believe, but it's not true. The last time I saw Meagan, she was already gone.

"You were seen driving through town with her. She was in the passenger seat. Everyone saw you two," he accuses, and he's not wrong. Everyone saw me driving with a hooded Meagan sitting still as death in the passenger seat of my dad's old 2000 black Chevy Cavalier, a car I haven't climbed into since the night the man made me drive him to the edge of town where he forced me to do the unthinkable.

Afterwards, he got out of my car, got into another car, and drove away into the night. I kept my eyes on my lap, just like he said to. All I wanted to do was go home, climb into bed, and forget it ever happened.

"Do you know how Meagan's phone ended up in the river?" Detective Shallitt asks.

Yes. I put her there. Wait a minute. He said phone. He didn't say anything about her body. What is going on? My breath catches. I try to stop my gut reaction, but it's too late. He saw my surprise. "I guess it was dropped off the bridge," I offer, but I barely know what I'm saying. It's like I'm on autopilot and someone else has stepped into my body. Meagan would be eating this up, I think to myself, and then I feel so ashamed. She loved games. She loved attention. She never knew when to quit. But that doesn't mean she deserved to be killed. Does it?

I lay my hands over my stomach as if I could cover the scrapes and the bruises from the cement cutting into me as I managed to drag her up over the bridge railing and drop her in the water. The fact that no one was there to see me is crazy. We live in a small town. There are only so many places to hang out. Wait a minute. I recall the smell of pot. Could someone else have been there? My brain is in hyperdrive. Who was there? What did they see? Did they take her body? Why else has this cop not mentioned it? He's supposed to have the evidence.

"How do you know that?" he demands. His voice is sharper than he intended. I can tell, but it's too late. ~~I shut down.~~ I force myself to focus on his question.

"It's a logical explanation, sir. If the phone was found at the river, someone must have dropped it there." I can't believe I'm talking to a cop in this manner. It's like Meagan has taken over my brain.

He leans forward. The look on his face says he's caught me. "I find it interesting that you said someone dropped it, which would mean you don't think she dropped it. Why would someone else have her phone, and what do you know about it?"

I white-knuckle the chair, even though I know it tells him I'm losing every sense of being calm, but that's because I am. I don't know how much longer I can sit here without falling apart. If she's not where I left her, then where is she? "I never said I knew anything."

"You also never said where you saw her last," he states. I know where I saw her last. It was at the river, but I can't tell him that. If I tell him that, it'll place me at the crime scene. I study his face a second too long, but it doesn't matter. He is as transparent as a closed book. He's not giving anything up. "I also find it interesting that your friend is missing, and you don't seem too concerned about finding her. Why is that?" he asks. He looks harmless enough as he sits in his chair, doing his job, mentally jabbing his fingers into my rib cage one at a time until I feel like I can't breathe. The look on his face tells me he laid a trap, and I walked right into it. *Dang it.* "Susan," he prompts.

I hold onto my silence. It's the only thing I've got left. "None of this is interesting to me," I insist, because it isn't. It's maddening. It's sleep-depriving. It's terrifying. But it is not interesting. "I saw her at the river," I say, because I did. "I guess she must have dropped the phone in there by accident," I add, because it's not a total lie. It could have fallen out of her pocket when she went over the railing, which is almost the same as her dropping the phone.

"Why would she do that?" he asks. "Why would she get rid of her phone?"

"Maybe she ditched it and hopped on the first bus out of town. Maybe she got on the 405 and just kept on going," I say, repeating the last theory I've heard more than a few times. It's strange how no one reached out to Meagan when she was here, but now that she's gone, everyone has an opinion about her absence.

"Do you believe that?" he asks. "Is she the type of girl who would do that sort of thing?"

"Meagan wasn't the typical girl," I say. I'm fighting a losing battle. The more questions he asks, the more agitated I become. I need out of here so I can try to find answers, even though I don't know where to start. "I guess she didn't want to be found," I mutter in a confused voice, because it's exactly how I feel.

"Why do you say that?" he asks again.

"There wasn't much she was afraid of."

"What was she afraid of?" he asks, making me wish I could rephrase my last statement.

"I don't know. She didn't tell me," I blurt.

"What did she tell you?" he asks. "Did she act as if she were some sort of trouble? Do you think someone is trying to hurt her?" he continues.

I bury my head in my hands, even though I know not looking at him makes me appear even more guilty. I force myself to look at him once more. "She told me nothing." This much is true. She was still as death. She couldn't talk. "She acted like nothing." This is also true. Her hood was up. I couldn't see her face. It was a sick game she'd just started in the last month, and she'd gotten way too good at it. I consider this now. Is there any way Meagan is still alive? Would she go *that far* to win the game?

"Was anyone trying to hurt her?" he repeats.

"Not that I know of," I say, answering only for last night. When I got in the car with her, the damage had already been done.

"What happened at the river?" he asks, and the first version of the truth forms in my mind.

"I don't know. I left her there," I answer.

His eyes widen. "You left your friend all by herself on the edge of town late at night with no way to get home," he accuses.

I say nothing. I can't. I'm crying and I can't stop. He gets up and walks out. Someone else enters the room. They sit in his chair.

"Susan."

"What?"

Sheriff Chatham's eyes stare into mine, scolding; but I'm so tired of answering for things I've done, things I can't talk about, because they're not things a fifteen-year-old girl would do. I had no choice.

I look over at the glass window. "I'm guessing you heard everything we just said, so I don't need to say it again," I say, but it comes out more like a demand.

"It's my job," he explains.

"Then you know who we're talking about, even if he doesn't,"

I continue. "She's *Meagan*, and you know as well as I do if she decides to do something, she does it." He opens his mouth and closes it again. This is so weird. I never thought I would be sitting at a table guarding myself against a man I've known pretty much my entire life. We're not related, but he feels like an uncle. Sheriff Chatham is the most consistent person I've ever known. He stands for everything that is right, good, and orderly. I wish he would stop staring at me like he's trying to pull thoughts out of my head. I can't let him in. I try and focus on the tiny letters and numbers pinned to his shirt—Badge 343.

"We had a fight earlier," I protest. It was a one-sided fight. I yelled at her. She didn't answer. "I was upset," I say, because I was petrified. There was a man sitting behind me in the car with a mask on. He had a gun. He told me not to look at him. He told me not to look at her. He told me to drive, and so I did. "I just started driving. I drove to the edge of town. When she was out of the car, I left," I say. "She had her phone with her the last I knew."

"So you didn't throw her phone in the water, and you have no idea where she is?" he replies.

"That is correct," I respond, because it is.

"And you weren't involved in any foul play at the bridge last night?" he asks as he taps a pencil on a clipboard.

I wasn't. It couldn't have been me who threw Meagan over. She was my best friend. The girl who tossed a body into the river was a girl under severe duress. A girl who had a gun pointed at her. A girl who was just doing what she was told to keep her family safe. I clear my throat. "I told you all I know," I offer, which is the truth.

He leans forward. "I know there's information you're not tellin' me. The longer you hold onto it, the worse it's gonna be for you. There is such a thing as obstruction of evidence," he threatens, but it doesn't scare me. Being an *accessory to murder* is much worse, and that's what I hold onto.

I grip the sides of my chair even harder in an attempt to keep it together. "I'm sorry. I've told you all I know" I say, even though I can't believe I'm lying to a person of the law.

"I'm merely statin' the facts, Susan, somethin' you haven't

done since I entered this room." He taps a finger on the table. "We know a third person was in that car when you were drivin' around. Who was it?" he asks.

"I don't know," I say, and it's the absolute truth.

"How long was this unknown person in your vehicle?" he asks.

Long enough to force me to drive downtown in plain sight of everyone so they all saw Meagan sitting beside me. Long enough to force me to throw her into the river. Long enough to frame me. I am so stupid. "I think I need a lawyer," I say.

6

My dad says I have to break up with you.

read Ryan's text as I walk out of the police station beside my mother three hours later.

RYAN:

He also says you should hire Sam DeVond. He's the best criminal defense lawyer in the state.

SUSAN:

Are we breaking up then? Thanks for the legal advice, but we already have a lawyer.

This is so weird. I never thought breaking up with a boy would involve legal language.

SUSAN:

How did your dad know I need a lawyer?

RYAN:

Everyone knows where you were this morning.
It's not exactly a secret.

Panic fills me all over again. Thanks to Meagan dividing my friend group over the past year or so, my list of friends is now pretty much nonexistent.

Susan: How is that even possible?

Ryan: Sarah's aunt works at the police station.

I hate Sarah. She was his girlfriend before me.

SUSAN:

So?

RYAN:

She told Molly's mom, who told Randy's mom,
who told my mom, and it just went around.

SUSAN:

I thought Molly's mom wasn't talking to Randy's
mom after what happened between her husband
and Randy's mom.

RYAN:

That's like old news, Susie. Geez.

I hate it when he calls me Susie. I only put up with it because he's on the football team, and he's popular, and I still can't believe he ever noticed me. That's all over now, and like many other sucky things in my life, it's all Meagan's fault. "Guess you got what you wanted. We broke up," I mutter under my breath.

I stare out the window.

"What?" Mom says. "You broke up with Ryan? Over this? Oh, honey. That's not a good idea. He was the one normal thing in your life right now."

I can't believe Mom's so stuck on worrying about Ryan and not me. I wish I was anywhere but here. Why can't Mom be on my side for once?

"I didn't break up with him, Mom. He broke up with me. His dad said he had to," I say, and then my lip quivers. I stop talking. I hate crying in front of Mom.

"Well, maybe when this is all over you two can get back together," Mom says in a cheery voice.

"You do realize Meagan is missing," I blurt. "Or worse," I mouth to the trees outside my window while trying to hold it together. Mom doesn't know what I haven't told her.

"I know, darling. But she's done this before. Remember? She'll come back," she answers too brightly. "And if she doesn't, she's almost sixteen. Lots of kids become independent at sixteen. Girls used to marry at that age," she muses.

"Yeah, well. This isn't some country song, Mother," I grump. "It's not like she's Loretta Lynn and she's going to marry some sicko pedophile, sing a bunch of songs, and make a bunch of money."

Mom sighs in her overly dramatic fashion. "I swear, Susan. I never should have let you watch that movie about Loretta's life. I thought it was inspiring. She came from nothing, and she made a name for herself. Only you girls and your raging feminism would turn it into something ugly," she accuses.

"I'm not a raging feminist, Mom. I'm merely pointing out she was a girl when she married a grown man. It's gross," I protest.

"Well, Loretta wasn't unhappy. She loved him. I don't know why it bothers you so much," she adds.

"It bothered Meagan," I say in a quiet voice. "Maybe there was another reason it bothered her," I continue.

"Stop trying to make sense of that girl's games, Susan. I used to think we could help her, but now that we're here, in the middle of this mess that might be the thing that pushes your father out the door, I just can't think about her anymore. I can't help her anymore. I have to think about my own family," Mom says before she breaks down in tears.

I've never seen her this way. I didn't know what to do. I still don't. Mom is the glue which holds us all together. If she loses it, who will be there for me?

We sit in the driveway in the minivan. Mom sits hunched over the steering wheel. I force myself to take her hand. "Mom. It's going to be okay. I'm sorry. I won't talk about her anymore, okay?"

She flings my hand off before turning to me with anger in her eyes. "Go talk to your father. He's the one who insisted you get a lawyer. He should be happy now."

I sit with her a few seconds longer, but she stares straight ahead. I open the van door and climb out. My eyes stray to the bedroom up above. The black curtains in Meagan's window are too still. I watch them a second longer, willing her tell-tale pale hand to pull them back so she can peek out, or for her palms to press themselves against the pane before she drags them down in an exaggerated way while she presses her face to the glass, as if she were in a horror movie and someone is killing her. But there is nothing. I walk up the steps and go inside.

"Why did you ask your mom to get you a lawyer?" Dad demands as he gets in my face.

"You told me to," I answer. "Well, you told Mom to," I correct myself.

"Of course, I did. I didn't think she would do it." He stares me down. "Why did you ask for a lawyer?"

I clear my throat. "Can we talk in your office?"

He doesn't answer except to pivot on his foot and stomp off. I follow him as close as I dare. I slide the door shut. "This isn't easy for me to say," I all but whisper.

"Sit down and tell me exactly what you told the sheriff," Dad demands. And so, I do. It's such a relief to have someone else take control.

After I finish, he leans back in his chair at his desk. "Is all of what you've said the truth?" he asks as he searches my face.

I open my mouth to tell him more but close it when I think of the man with the gun. "Yes," I say.

"You really don't know where Meagan is?" he questions.

"No," I say easily, because it's the truth.

We sit there in silence for a bit longer. He stares up at the ceiling. "Do you think she wants you to come find her?" he asks.

I blink in surprise. "Why do you say that?"

He drops his pen on the desk between us. "She was always playing games, Sue. Do you think this is just another one of those games?" he asks in earnest.

My face flushes. "I didn't know you knew," I say quietly.

He groans. "I'm sure there's a lot I still don't know. I don't know how much I want to know, but I am your father. I do know some things." He points a finger at me. "I knew that girl was trouble from day one. I should have listened to my instinct. I should never have let your mother keep her," he said, as if Meagan was a family pet.

I'm so confused. "You asked Mom to let her stay, and she did it for me. Meagan was my friend," I offer. My eyes fill with tears once more.

Dad sighs, making me feel like I know nothing. I hate it. "It was a suggestion, Susan. I didn't think your mother would actually do it. Anyway, don't blame yourself. Your mom is not as heroic as you think. She did it for herself. Becoming a foster parent was like a huge pat on the back for her. It was her way of saying 'look what I'm doing. Look how much I'm giving of myself,'" he says bitterly.

His animosity toward Mom slaps me in the face. I had no idea he was so unhappy. "I don't believe you," I accuse. I know how much Mom sacrificed to try to help Meagan and look what she got in return. "Are you going to leave us?" I ask.

A guilty look crosses his face. I want to cry. "Why would you say that?" he asks.

I stare him down. He didn't say no. He answered my question with a question. "You're not the only one who can read people," I say cryptically. I stand up and walk back and forth. "I told Mom I wouldn't talk about Meagan anymore to her. I don't want to upset her more than I already have," I offer.

Dad throws his hands in the air. "Well. You know where I am. This talk doesn't upset me." He drops a fisted hand on the desk. "If that girl is hiding, we're going to find her. She's up to something, I can tell you that. You're not taking the fall for her, and neither are we," he vows as I walk toward the door. "She's probably not hiding. She probably ran away. If she did, there's nothing we can do about it."

His strange words don't match his tone. I wish he didn't sound so happy about the possibility that she ran. I wish I could tell him what I know. It's on the tip of my tongue, but something holds me back, and it's not just the guy with the gun. If I tell Dad what I know, it will only get me grounded. Then he won't let me go anywhere, and I'll never get closer to finding her. "Hey, pumpkin." His voice is slightly warmer. "Where are you going? You got a hot date?" he teases, but I know his heart's not in it. Dad's been acting different toward me ever since I started dating.

My eyes water. My throat tightens. "No. Ryan says he has to break up with me," I say.

"Just as well. That kid was a bit of a turd, if you ask me," Dad says, surprising me.

"He's on the football team, Dad. He's popular," I protest.

"That doesn't mean he's not a turd," Dad replies. "He's definitely not good enough for my daughter," he adds.

I can't help but smile. At least he didn't praise Ryan like Mom did. "You think every boy's not good enough for me," I whine, but secretly I love Dad's loyalty.

"That's because they aren't," he announces.

I study him a little longer. "Do you have any idea where Meagan might be?" I ask.

Something flickers in his eyes, something I can't name. He knows something. And he's trying to hide it from me. What does he know?

"I don't, but if I did, I wouldn't tell you. You need to stay away from that girl. She's dangerous," he growls.

"Right," I say. All I want is to get out of here. I can hardly look him in the eye. If he only knew what I'm capable of, it's not Meagan he'd be worried about.

I race upstairs to my room. I sit in my windowsill and stare out at the street. "Where are you, Meagan?" I ask before turning my phone off silent. So many questions run through my mind. Who took her body, and why? The guy with the gun wouldn't, would he? Why would he make me throw her over if he was just going to go back for her? It doesn't make any sense. I force down the vomit long enough to get to the bathroom. I can't believe she's dead, but she has to be. I saw her. I felt her limp, dead weight as I dragged her over the cement.

A photo pops up on my screen. The white bottoms of Meagan's shoes light up the night just like my signature pale yellow hoodie which I shoved into the bottom of my closet after I got home. "I know what you did" is attached to the photo. "And soon everyone else will too."

I clutch my phone to my chest as I climb into the bathtub. I sit beneath the windowpane and wonder, What if he's out there? What if he's watching me right now? My chest feels tight. I close my eyes and try to count. "You are breathing, you are breathing," I mouth the words silently as I try to take deep, calming breaths. It almost works, but then I check my phone again. I can't stop staring at the bottom of her white tennis shoes. "Who sent this? What does it mean?" I whisper as tears ran down my cheeks. I need help. I can't handle any of this alone for one more second. I wrack my brain. I can't text Ryan. He just broke up with me. I can't talk to Meagan. She's gone. I bump my head against the window frame just enough to make my head ring. I bite my lip so hard I taste blood. My fingers dig into my thighs. I think I'm going crazy.

"Who can I text?" I whisper before snapping the first person who pops into my head, Jaz. She was so nice to me at the party the other night. "Hey, girl. Got a min?" I ask, trying to sound all cool, like I even know what that means.

"Sorry. Busy. 4-Ever," she answers.

Her response is so cruel. I'm so shook I almost drop my phone on the bottom of the porcelain bathtub. I'm so stupid. Whatever issue has Jaz with me, I'm sure it's tied to Meagan. I can't believe I let her isolate me like this. There was a short time in junior high we had a group of friends. There were eight of us. But it didn't take long for Meagan to split us all up. I didn't see what she was doing at the time. I thought everyone was being mean to her. I didn't see everything clearly until it was too late. Everyone told me I shouldn't stick up for her, that she was toxic, but I didn't listen. All I could see was her pain from losing her parents. I didn't want to believe she was that cruel. I thought she was just acting out. Now I'm not so sure.

I sit in the same place for far too long, but I can't make myself move. I'm crying my eyes out when my phone lights up. I wipe at my eyes and try to focus as I look down. "Hey. Are you okay?" Conrad asks.

"No," I said.

"Can I come over?"

I'm tempted to say "yes." If he comes over, I won't be alone in whatever this is. But if I say yes, I have to deal with Conrad Barnes, the brainiac boy whose one claim to fame was solving a hundred-year-old mystery tied to the town we lived in at the age of eleven. He is as strange as the discovery he made. He's also my first kiss, but that's just because he was kind of famous and I wanted to know what it would be like to kiss someone famous. At least that's what I told myself. I was almost thirteen, so it shouldn't count. "I don't know if that's a good idea."

"Why not?" he asks, and I can't help but smile. Conrad may be a bit awkward, but at least he gets answers.

"I'm a hot mess," I type, and then delete it. I hold my phone to my mouth and hit record. "I'm not ready for you to come over. I dumped a body off a bridge because I was being held at gunpoint, but now she's nowhere to be found. It's been forty-eight hours. No one is looking for her. All they're worried about is her broken phone. Why aren't they looking for her?" I say into the microphone before hitting the delete button. Sending him a voice message feels too personal, but I can't write anything incriminating. "It's not a good time," I type and send before bursting into hysterical giggles that make me feel like a crazy person.

"Meagan. Where are you?" I whisper while staring at the closed closet door in the bathroom. I know she's gone, but I'm not ready to accept it. Why haven't they found her body? I'd give anything for that door to fall open and find tiny, dark-haired Meagan standing there like a weirdo zombie staring unblinkingly

33

at me with a deranged look on her face, like only Meagan does. She's way too good at being creepy, and a huge fan of horror movies.

My mind returns to the threats the man made about exposing me. He had to be the one who sent me the strange text. Who else would have been down there to take the picture? He's not going to post it. He can't. If he posts it, he reveals himself. Why would he risk that? Is Meagan with him? Why would he keep a dead body?

The words *dead body* bounce around in my head like a mantra. I can't shut it off. I'm cold everywhere, and it isn't from the tub.

"Susan," Mom yells.

I crawl out of the unforgiving bathtub and walk across the floor. Everything feels so surreal. It's like someone else's hand turns the doorknob and enters the hallway. I walk downstairs like a zombie. "Susan," Mom says in a sharper tone. It almost sounds like she's scared.

"What."

"I asked you what you want for supper."

My mind swims. It feels so wrong to be eating when Meagan is gone. I stare at the empty dining room table. The thought of three plates being there instead of four is so cruel. "Are we going somewhere?"

She forces a smile. "That's a great idea. Would you like to go out to eat, Jeff?"

"Do we have to go inside?" he yells from the corner of his study. Dad's chair sits in the corner. It's no coincidence his desk sits in the back corner closest to the wall. Mom doesn't like closed doors. Dad doesn't like feeling a zoo animal. I pretend to be oblivious to his calculated hiding place and Mom's eternal searching. Meagan's absence isn't the only elephant in the room.

Mom's mouth opens as if to speak. I prepare myself to wait another hour before we go anywhere. Any second Mom's going to start lecturing us about not eating in the car because it takes away from family time. The real issue is she can't stand the thought of anyone getting crumbs in her pristine minivan, which is absurd. It's not like it's a Bentley. I thought the whole purpose of a boring minivan is because it's a mom car. Aren't mom cars supposed to house messy children with pride?

Mom claps her hands. "Okay. Let's have a car picnic," she announces, and that's when I know we've all entered an alternate universe. There are so many thoughts inside my head that want to come out. Like, why did it take Meagan possibly dying to make Mom less of an ogre about her damn car? Or why did it take Meagan dying for Mom to act like she's excited about having a family outing with just the three of us?

I can't think of anything to say, and so I nod my head and try not to stare at Mom like like she's grown a second head.

She claps her hands again. "Okay. Okay. Jeff," she yells, and her voice is so shrill.

"What, Nell?" he barks in the same tone.

Mom winces at his response. I feel so bad for her.

"Jeff. If you don't want to go, Susan and I will go by ourselves. We can bring you something back." Her voice waivers, and I wonder, is Mom going to cry? What is going on? She never cries. She clears her throat. "I'd really like it if you would come."

The only thing worse than hearing Mom practically beg is waiting for my jerk of a father to answer her. He's so nice to me, but then he turns around and acts like that to her. I could choke on the resentment between them.

I catch Mom's wounded expression in the corner of my eye while looking at her and pretending not to look at her. It's so awkward. I don't want to go eat. I'm not hungry. I just want to go to my room, except I don't. All it does is remind me that Meagan's not there.

The house is too quiet. Ever since Meagan left, a sense of calm has crossed our threshold. It covers the walls, floats in the halls, hovers in the dark empty spaces, and it haunts me. It's like I've longed for it for so long, and now that it's here, I hate it. All I want is for Meagan and the bundle of teenage angst she wore like a badge of honor to return. It's like she didn't know how to be anything but conflicted, frustrated, angry, sullen, pouty, and dissatisfied all at once, all the time. It was exhausting, but it was addictive.

She was so unpredictable. I never knew how much of it was for real, or if it was all for show. She spent a lot of time cutting everyone down. Even though it was spot on, it wasn't funny. I always thought she was just bitter because she didn't have any parents or family, but now I don't know.

When she did say something nice, it was as if it hurt her to speak the words aloud, and then I would feel bad for thinking that, which was just dumb. The more I think about how much of my emotions depended on Meagan, the more withdrawn I feel. It's like I needed her existence to know who I was, which is so messed up. If Meagan were here, she would tell me how lame I am for letting another person control me, even if that other person was her. But she's not here to yell at me. It sucks.

I've gone over that night so many times in my mind, wondering what I could have done differently. Could I have saved her from the man with the gun? Should I have gone over the bridge railing with her? Could I have dragged her body to shore without drowning? I was so scared. Everything was dark, inside and out. All I could think of was his gun, and what he told me to do, and what he was going to do with me next if I didn't do exactly what he said to do. I was terrified. I was so sure she was dead. She had to be dead. There was no way she would go over that railing if she wasn't dead. Right?

I wish I could believe this is all a game. I wish I could stop worrying about Meagan. I wish I never saw the man with the gun. I wish I had never gotten in the car with her. I want everything to go back to when she was giving me the silent treatment. I thought Meagan's dirty looks in the school hallways were torture. I thought hiding out in the girl's bathroom crying was the worst thing she could make me do. I shake my head to clear it of these terrible thoughts about her. She's gone. It doesn't matter what she did before. I don't wish her dead. What kind of monster would that make me?

I still can't believe Jaz was so rude to me in her last text. She could have just said she was busy. She didn't need to be so snotty. She knows Meagan. She knows what she can be like. Jaz is a lot like Meagan. She just hides it better. Instead of sneering at me and saying rude things, Jaz usually puts people down in other ways. She has perfected the skill of carefully constructed criticism.

I remember the day Jaz smiled at me while pointing a perfectly manicured nail at a flyer I made for a school event. We were on the same planning committee. "The boxes aren't big enough for the stamp to fit in. It's going to look ridiculous. You made it all wrong." My stomach started to hurt. All I wanted was to be somewhere else. Away from her and her cutting comments.

Suddenly, a middle finger jabbed at the same piece of paper that Jaz's hand rested on. "Didn't you just say a second ago no one keeps these pieces of paper anyway? Didn't you say they throw them in the trash," Meagan demanded in a tone that could only be taken as extremely confrontational.

"Yeah, so? They still need to look nice. I guess I just like things done right," Jaz said.

Meagan snorted. "No, you don't. You like to tell other people what to do so you can come along and tell them how they did it wrong." She crossed her arms over her chest and stared Jaz down. I couldn't believe what was happening. No one stands up to Jaz, who rolled her big brown eyes.

"Whatever, Mazie. I don't know why you care. You're not on the planning committee."

Meagan leaned in even closer to Jaz, getting all up in her space. "My name is *Meagan*, which I know you know, because I've heard you say it countless times to your friends when you're talking about me behind my back. So don't *pretend* you don't know my name. The only thing you're right about is that I'm not involved in anything you're tied to. Committees are *super lame*, but I'd be willing to form one called '50 ways Jaz can suck it.'"

I remember choking down laughter. I couldn't believe Meagan said that to Jaz, or how Jaz's eyes bugged because she couldn't believe what she had just heard. Meagan's hand flew to her hip. She raised her chin, narrowed her eyes, and looked down her nose at Jaz, mirroring Jaz's mean-girl stance.

"Now why don't you get outta our way so we can go hand out these killer flyers Susan made for your stupid event that no one will come to anyway. I'll be sure and tell everybody how *wonderful* of a time they'll have listening to you lecture them about things that don't matter, like how to make a proper flyer." Meagan wadded one up and threw it at Jaz, hitting her square in the face. "If you don't like how other people do things, then shut your bitchy mouth and do it yourself. *Most people* know the proper thing to do is just say 'Thank you.'"

I remember how my heart sang. I couldn't believe someone had told Jaz off. It was unheard of. And that someone was my friend. I'd never had anyone stand up for me at school before, and especially not another girl.

I stood there feeling so awkward. I wanted to share in Meagan's moment of triumph, but Jaz wouldn't leave. She stood there frozen and blinking. Meagan snuck her arm through mine and shoved the flyers across the table at Jaz. "*Actually*, you can do what you want with them. Susan did the hard part. She created them and she printed them. If you don't like them, fix them yourself."

I let myself be led by Meagan across the room and out the nearest door. "You're crazy," I said as soon as we were out of Jaz's sight. "She's not gonna forget what you did."

Meagan just laughed out loud. "Good. I hope she doesn't. She might look like a twig but she's a bully."

We bumped shoulders as we walked along. It felt so strange. It wasn't like Meagan to let anyone get that close to her. "Yeah. She's something," I said. "So, are you gonna like come to my event?" I hate how uncertain I sounded.

"Will there be any hot guys there?" Meagan joked.

"It's at our school, so…"

She sighed all dramatically. "I suppose I'll have to come. You gotta have some *cool factor* to bring others in."

"Thanks," I said, and I really meant it. I was a little nervous about what Jaz might do to me since Meagan had humiliated her so thoroughly, but Jaz had started it. Not Meagan. Meagan was just defending me because I was too much of a wimp to stand up for myself.

"Susan," Mom's voice interrupted my thoughts.

"What?"

"What do you want? She's waiting."

I look out the car window. How did we get to the drive thru so quickly? How did I not notice? I hardly remember getting in the car. I scan the lit-up menu for the drive thru, trying to focus, but all I can think of is Meagan. She would order a hamburger with bacon and cheese and tots. Then she'd order some kind of banana ice cream thing and she'd dip her tots in the ice cream. She would hold the tomato, onion, lettuce, and mustard. I asked her once why she didn't just order a plain hamburger with ketchup and pickle, and she would grin and tell me, "It's more fun to list what they can't put on it."

I stare harder at the board, trying to focus while ignoring Mom's head cranked to stare at my face. "I want a junior chicken wrap and a junior vanilla mixer with M&Ms," I yell in the direction of Dad's driver side rolled-down window.

"Stop yelling in my ear," Mom orders in a quiet voice from the passenger seat.

"She's not yelling," Dad fires back.

"Why didn't you sit behind Dad?" Mom asks. "It would have been easier to order."

I look over at the empty seat which should be Meagan's. She had a thing about sitting behind the driver. I don't know what it was. I only knew I didn't dare sit in her space. It was just easier that way.

"Nell," Dad says before I can say anything.

I turn and look out my window. Tears roll down my cheeks.

"What?" Mom replies.

Sometimes I don't understand. I thought Moms had intuition. Mom was the one who insisted Meagan stay for as long as she needed to, but it was always Dad who saw everything for what it was. Like now, as he glances in my direction and then turns back around, clearing his throat. "I like you sitting there, Susie. It makes sense."

It's an olive branch, and I take it. But inside, I want to break the thing in half and throw it at both of them. How in the hell am I supposed to act normal when my best friend is missing or dead? And I know his words are a peace offering, but nothing makes any sense. It's strange that neither of them will say a word about Meagan. It's so weird that they're trying to act like everything is normal. It's weird that there have been no news headlines about a girl who should be considered missing. The police brought me in and questioned me, so why isn't there anyone out there looking for Meagan? Why isn't there some sort of Amber alert on our phones? Why didn't the local news pick up this story? Is it because she's a foster kid? Does no one care?

I know a man threatened me, but no one else does. So why isn't anyone asking more questions?

Soon enough we're home. Mom and Dad return to their separate corners of the house. I trudge up the stairs thinking about Meagan with every step I take. Maybe if I pretend this is another one of her games, I'll have better luck finding some kind of clue. I can't sit still and do nothing.

I go over every conversation I had with her in the past few weeks that I can recall for the hundredth time, as I sit on the floor of my room, leaning against the door. My brain is exhausted, but then a memory takes me by surprise. We've had so many fights over the past month, I was shoving them from my mind, because I knew another one would happen soon enough. It seemed like every little thing set her off.

The last one was the worst. I'd come home, and she was in my closet. I was so mad because Meagan had just lectured me about going into her closet and there she was in mine. I screamed at her and ignored the scared look on her face, because it was easier that way. It looked sincere but I was so tired of dealing with all her drama. All the time. It was exhausting.

I get up and open my closet door. I shine my phone light all around but don't see anything out of place. I'm down on my hands and knees searching. I have no idea what I'm looking for. I'm about ready to give up when I spy a corner of paper sticking out of the very back corner of the closet. I lay down on my stomach, cursing Meagan the entire time because I hate spiders and I can't believe she would go so far as to cram something into a dark, hidden place in my room. Except that I can.

I open the small bound book that looks like some sort of journal. I turn the page.

Dear Diary,

I'm not sure what to write. I am a girl without a past, at least that's what I was told. But how do I forget every memory I've ever known, and why would I want to? Is it fair that I have to trade one horrible memory for so many good ones? It doesn't seem right.

It's not right that one awful accident stole my mom from me. I'm just a girl. I'm eleven-and-a-half years old. How do I sit at a supper table and pretend everything is normal when my head and heart feel like they're exploding?

They tell me to hold on, but I have nothing to hold onto. They tell me that things will get better. All I know is they can't get worse.

They watch me and pretend they aren't. I wear my mask because it's what they expect. I hold in my tears. I force a smile at the appropriate times. This is my life now. My life is just a stupid joke, like the name of the town I've been sent to in the middle of nowhere, Iowa.

I know because I looked it up after meeting the strange, old woman who lives in her creepy little house on the edge of town. The cop stopped there to talk to her on the front porch. She tried to take me inside so I could use the bathroom, but he said no. Even though she was kind of scary, I wanted to talk to her longer. She's the first person I've met here who doesn't watch me as if I'm about to do something awful. She asked me how old I was, and *if I liked oatmeal cookies. She told me she had a daughter once. The cop glared at her when she talked about her daughter, but she ignored him. I wish I were that brave. I think I could be. It just takes practice.*

Many of the words on the page are blurry, as if someone cried over them. I read over it again, thinking. Did Meagan write these words? And if she did, was she really almost twelve, or is this just another part of her sick game?

I turn the page.

Dear Diary,

I suppose I should date my entries, but I don't want to. The only way to keep going is to not think about time, or place, or the last time I saw them. I hate, hate, hate, that the girl I live with HAS to be my friend. I wish I could unhear what her mother said about the two of us being friends. Why did I have to go back for a stupid pencil when I know there's a whole box of them in the room I share with the girl I thought was my best friend? But now I know the truth. Our friendship isn't real. It's all a lie like everything else.

For a few days I thought I finally found one thing real in this whole mess, but I was wrong about that too. Mom was right about that too. She told me once the only person I could depend on was myself, but it's so hard. I get so tired. I want to be like the rest of them. I want my biggest fear to be if my green shoes match the green stripes on my hoodie. I want to giggle when J smiles at me with his crooked tooth that sticks out just the right way in front of the others. I like his messy hair, his brown eyes, and the freckles on his nose.

But I can't smile back at J. I can't get too close. Everyone I get close to is taken away. J doesn't deserve that. But the girl who is friends with me because she has to be, well, she better watch her back.

My stomach tightens as I read the first paragraph again. Tears roll down my cheeks. No wonder Meagan drew me in, shoved me away, and blew up my friendships. She thought I didn't like her. I could almost see why she was so angry, but why didn't she just tell me what my mom said instead of being pissed at me for four years?

The faceless man with the gun interrupts my thoughts. I can't believe I didn't even try to see any part of him. I was so scared. I think of the possibility of Meagan pretending she was dead. Why would she do that to me? Did the gunman threaten her, too, or are they in it together?

I start questioning everything all over again. Who is the gunman to Meagan? What if they're friends? What if they were pulling a trick on me? I think of the night at the bridge. I can't believe I lifted her body up onto that railing and rolled her over. It had to be the adrenaline and the fear which gave me the strength. Other fears filled me; if she's alive, she's definitely not going to talk to me. I tossed her off a freaking bridge. Wait a minute, if she's alive then she knows I was being ordered at gunpoint. And if she's alive, she was the one who was playing dead in the seat beside me and on the bridge. She went over the railing without a fight. She let me think she was gone.

I return to her journal entries. Who was J? My mind draws a blank. Maybe he's from her old school, but she made it sound like he was from the school we went to together. There was a Jack, but he had black hair and green eyes, and I think he moved away before I knew her. There was a Jeremy, but his eyes were green. He didn't really pay attention to girls until last year. I have no idea who J was, but does it really matter? He has nothing to do with what's going on now.

Dear Diary,

I hate Amber Rollins. She is so, so stupid. I don't know why Susan wants to be her friend so bad. Amber is mean. She doesn't want to be anyone's friend. She just wants to know stuff about them so she can make fun of them, like she made fun of Susan for being my friend because she feels sorry for me and because Susan's parents get money for keeping me at their house. Because I'm a foster kid.

If Amber didn't want me to write down what she said about all her friends and shove those hate notes in their bags, she shouldn't talk so loud. She should learn to keep her big mouth shut.

I never would have told Amber the only reason she has friends is because she has the nicest house, a big TV, and yummy food if she hadn't dragged me into the bathroom and practically spit in my face while telling me the only reason I was at her house was because she felt sorry for me and her mother made her invite me. But sometimes the truth hurts, and Amber knows that more than anyone. Going to her house was supposed to be fun. It was my first all-girl sleepover, but Amber ruined it, and so I decided to ruin her.

I hate Amber Rollins. I'm not sorry I was as mean as I have ever been. Susan should have known we wouldn't have any fun if we went to Amber's stupid party.

I lay the diary down. It's so hard reading what Meagan wrote. It hurts to see all that emotion in her writing. I guess I understand why she was so angry all the time. She was already hurting and then someone hurt her more. Even though I get where she's coming from, Meagan was so exhausting.

I remember the invite from Amber to her birthday sleepover like it was yesterday. I was so excited it took me a second or two to realize Meagan's name wasn't on it. I felt bad at the time because I was excited to go somewhere without her, but I didn't feel bad enough to not go. I wasn't about to ask Amber if Meagan could come, because I was afraid Amber would tell me to stay home.

My stomach hurts when the memory of that event hits me like a brick. I didn't realize how much I missed the old times when everything was simple, before Meagan moved into my house, my room, and my life.

It was my mother who called Amber's mom and guilted her into inviting Meagan to the sleepover a few days before. Things quickly went downhill once Amber was forced to invite Meagan. Amber was absolutely awful to me at school every chance she got, but I was determined to go to her sleepover, so I put up with it. Her sleepovers were the event of the year. Any girl who was anyone went to Amber's slumber party.

The sleepover was miserable. Amber was as mean as a snake, like Meagan said she'd be. Every girl got a goodie bag except for me. The fact that Meagan took everything out of her own bag and destroyed it in front of everyone hardly made me feel better. I ended up sleeping outside of the circle of sleeping bags the girls created. When we woke up, I was shocked to find everyone's sleeping bag had an obscenity written on it in black sharpie except for mine. Meagan was nowhere to be found. Most of the girls scowled at me, but quiet, mysterious Charla was cool as always. She stood there silently with a small smile on her face that told me she knew everything that went down, but I knew she had no part in it. I didn't know what to do so I rolled up my sleeping bag, walked downstairs, and asked Amber's mom to call my mom and then I went outside and sat on the front steps to wait.

I stare at the open diary. I still can't believe Meagan is missing.

I can't believe Mom isn't wondering where she is. What if Mom knows what happened to her? What if mom is hiding something from me? That would be crazy, wouldn't it? It all feels like such madness. I need to talk to someone, or else I'm going to lose it.

I pick up my phone and Snap the last person I talked to besides Meagan. I try to look in the phone without crying, but it's no use. When I think of Ryan dumping me and Meagan maybe being dead, I can't help it. The tears start to fall. I take a picture anyway. "Ryan, please answer. I need you," I type before sending the Snap.

The minutes drag by as I sit there with my phone in hand. Waiting. I think of Meagan's phone and everything we wrote each other over the past week or two. I try to remember if there was anything incriminating on there, but she was the one who was always writing strange cryptic messages. Not me. She was the one who would get all dramatic and make crazy accusations and threats. Half the time she was kidding, the other half, I was never sure. Her sense of humor was way too dark, but I couldn't get her to stop, and I knew she would never come close to doing what she said, like when she said, "Wouldn't it be funny if we stole Amber's beautiful new Jeep and lit it on fire just to watch it burn?"

My brain hurts when I try to think if I ever sent her anything crazy back. I don't think I did, but still, I blush at the thought of a cop or a detective reading our crazy exchanges. Most of the time they were SnapChat and I don't think they can bring that back. My phone vibrates in my hand. It's Ryan. I can't believe he answered. My heart races, which was just stupid, because we're not together. I open the Snap. He looks so done with me.

RYAN:

Stop snapping me. I'm talking to someone else now. We r thru. U r pathetic.

I try not to be too upset, but he doesn't have to be so jerky to me.

SUSAN:

I'm not upset about us, Ryan. It's about M.
Something happened. She's missing.

RYAN:

Whatever, he answers. She's just seeking attn.

SUSAN:

No. It's more than that. She went over the bridge
into the river.

RYAN:

WTF? Ru kidding? That's not funny.

SUSAN:

Why would I joke about that? They found her
phone. They didn't find her.

RYAN:

Who?

SUSAN:

The cops.

RYAN:

How do u know all this?

I know I shouldn't be telling him everything, but I have to tell
someone, and my parents don't want to hear it.

SUSAN:

U know how. You know they took me downtown.

RYAN:

Y did they take u d?

SUSAN:

Because I'm her friend.

I'm not ready to tell him what they accused me of. I wait for a response. I don't get anything. It feels like forever as I stare at my phone, but I can't do anything but wait.

RYAN:

They can't take u in w/o a reason. What did u do?

SUSAN:

More than I'm telling them.

I feel like a criminal. I can't believe I'm trying to impress my ex-boyfriend when I'm in serious trouble. I really am a terrible person.

RYAN:

What does that mean?

SUSAN:

I went to my car. She was in the passenger seat. She was acting like she was dead.

RYAN:

Y would she do that?

I let out a sigh and type.

SUSAN:

U no y.

RYAN:

Nvm. U r right. Then what?

SUSAN:

Then I got mad because we had just broken up.

I hiccup and kind of hold in a sob. I take a deep breath.

SUSAN:

I was mad, and I yelled at her when I got in the car and sat in the driver seat, but she didn't do anything. She had her hood up and she was sitting there. All still and stuff.

RYAN:

That's so weird.

I feel a tiny bit better. I'm not the only one who thinks her strange act is super-creepy.

SUSAN:

I stopped yelling and then a man said something from the back seat.

RYAN:

No way. Did u freak?

Susan:

Duh. He said he had a gun and to not turn around. He told me to drive. So I did.

RYAN:

You're making this up.

SUSAN:

I wish I was.

RYAN:

What r u going to do?

SUSAN:

I don't know. I'm not sure what I can do.

RYAN:

This is serious.

SUSAN:

I know. The cops found her phone but not her.

RYAN:

That's weird.

I don't think he wants to ask me if I know more about everything, and for some dumb reason, this makes me angry. It was like no one wants to know the truth. Except me. I know more truth than anyone else because I was there, but none of that helps me.

"Ask me what happened," I whisper at my phone screen, but it doesn't.

RYAN:

What do u have to do with her phone?

SUSAN:

They wanted to know if I knew how it got in the water.

RYAN:

And do u?

SUSAN:

Yes

I hit send.

I think the reason I'm enjoying stringing him along is because now he has to pay attention to me, something he used to do before he dumped me. I start to type some more.

SUSAN:

I know because...

RYAN:

Gonna go hang with the guys. TTYL. I'll be on D&D.

I cancel my Snap and stare at my phone. I can't believe he left me hanging like that. After everything I just told him. He still left me on red.

My phone vibrates again. It's restricted. I open it.

I can't believe you threw me over.

I catch my breath. My stomach hurts. I think I'm going to puke all over again. It has to be Meagan.

SUSAN:

I had to. You know. You were there. You would have done the same.

MEAGAN:

I wouldn't have.

SUSAN:

I thought you were gone. Forever.

MEAGAN:

Is that a reason to pitch me in the river?

Now that I know she's alive, thinking of her playing dead infuriates me. She can't be in that much distress, or she wouldn't be texting me.

SUSAN:

Where are you?

MEAGAN:

Nowhere you'll find me, not that you'd come looking.

SUSAN:

I'm sorry.

MEAGAN:

Whatever.

I almost laugh. Even though it's such a cliché answer, it was her favorite one. Depending on the day, sometimes that was the only answer I got no matter what I said to her. One thing I can say about knowing Meagan, it was never boring.

SUSAN:

You're the one who acted like you were dead. All you had to do was say something. Like IDK, I'm alive. Don't throw me over.

I taunt about the time I wonder what exactly she wants. She wouldn't be texting me unless she was after something. I have no idea what's coming next.

MEAGAN:

I couldn't speak, and you know why.

I bite my lip. I can't believe I'm being so callous, but I can't help it. I have nothing to lose, but too much to gain. I really don't want my dad to move out or my parents to split up.

SUSAN:

How are you texting me now if you're in danger?

I ask, knowing she may not talk to me ever again, but I have to know. I can't get anywhere without knowing what she will do next. It's all so frustrating. She's still controlling me, and I'm still letting her, but I can't stop caring about her safety. Someone has to, and no one else will.

MEAGAN:

Who says I'm not in danger?

SUSAN:

I say.

MEAGAN:

You don't know everything.

SUSAN:

Then enlighten me.

I don't know what she wants me to do for her, or what she thinks I can do that I probably can't because the man threatened me, and she knows that. When I remember that, it makes me mad all over again.

SUSAN:

Are you with him?

MEAGAN:

Sometimes we can't choose who we're with.

So many awful thoughts fill my mind, and I start crying.

SUSAN:

Is he hurting you?

MEAGAN:

Not physically. Gotta go.

It's super annoying. All I can think is Ryan ran out on me, and she's doing the same thing.

My eyes water. I'm so relieved she's alive. It has to be her. No one would text me and pose as her, would they? What would they have to gain from doing that? She didn't ask me for any information. She didn't ask me for anything. That's weird. She didn't tell me anything specific that told me I was really talking to Meagan either, because I didn't ask. I should have asked.

I breathe a little easier. I want to ask her more about who she's with, but I can't, because the more I know, the more danger I'm in. I should ask her if she needs anything. I should have asked her what I can do for her. I should say something instead of sitting here staring at my phone like an idiot. But I'm hurt too. I can't believe she let me think she was dead. I'm sure no matter what happened or why, she brought it on herself. She was never looking out for me, no matter how much I wish she was. The Meagan I know only knows how to help herself.

7

Badge 343

read over my notes I made from my interview with Susan Tripp, and I'm just as frustrated as the first three times I read them. She gave me nothing. I lean back in my chair. "She's been runnin' around with Meagan too long. She's startin' to act like her."

"Talking to yourself again, Chatham?" Laurel questions.

I throw my hands around. "You know me. I'm just processin'."

She laughs as she leans against the corner of my desk. "Percolating, huh?"

I tap my fingertips against each other. "Somethin' like that."

"What're you working on?" she says, and I drop a blank piece of paper on top of the file. Laurel works the phones, and she's been known to gossip.

"O'Reilly," she mutters, like a curse word. She shakes her head back and forth. "Some things never change."

Her contempt catches me off guard. Laurel is always so bubbly and friendly, to the point that sometimes it's a little hard to take dependin' on what kind of day I've had. She stands up and walks out without another word. I fiddle with the corner of the file.

"That was heavy," Shawn says from across the room, but he's headed my way. I kind of wish he wouldn't. I've known Shawn since we were kids, just like Laurel. There's comfort in stayin' in a town where you know everyone and everyone knows you, until somethin' like this happens, and people's true feelin's come out of the woodwork. Shawn plops down in a chair and rolls until he bumps into me. We're shoulder-to-shoulder. "You know she had a thing for you."

"Who? Marlena?" I ask. The hope in my voice is ridiculous.

He laughs. I want to punch him in the face. "No. Laurel."

"But she was a freshman when I was a senior. I barely knew her," I protest.

"Doesn't matter. You were captain of the football team and the debate team, and you were the lead in every school play. You were the homecoming king. What more is there to say?"

His reluctant praises of my high-school accomplishments feel so strange. "Those things weren't a big deal to me."

He laughs, but it's more like a bark. "Of course not. But they were to everybody else. Trust me. Lots of guys in your position would have taken advantage of that shit."

His words make me angry. "I guess I'm not most guys."

His eyes narrow. "Nope. You're like Mother Theresa, except you're a man."

"Does this conversation have a point?"

He stares me down. "Why are you lookin' up Marlena O'Reilly? Everyone knows she left town the night she flipped out and tried to kill old Hammy Harris and she ain't been back since." He crosses his arms on his chest. "'Sides, I thought you were supposed to be workin' on findin' that foster girl for Jeff Tripp." He gives me a sly grin, and I know he's about to say somethin' I don't wanna hear. "He's a bit of a cold fish, but that wife of his, she's a little firecracker." He nudges me in the side with his elbow. "If you know what I'm sayin'."

I give him a hard shove. He almost falls off his chair. "Why don't you get back to work insteada fillin' my ears with a bunch of nonsense. All that's in the past, and I don't know why you can't leave it there. They're just a bunch of ugly rumors made up by a bunch of small-town gossips who have nothin' better to do than sit around makin' up stuff about people they don't know."

Shawn gets up from his chair. Somethin' in his stare has me on my feet. He shoves me back. "Careful, Deputy. Don't cross that line," I warn.

He sniffs. "You crossed it first, *Sheriff*." He takes a few steps backwards, but I sense he's not done. "I find it interesting that you are always defending the O'Reilly women. Everyone knows they're trash."

It's so easy to see my fist break his nose. I can even hear it crack. But I'm a professional, and I always do the right thing. That's my fatal flaw. That, and I have to keep my job because I have bills to pay. I'm twenty-eight years old. I'm not movin' back into my mother's house. Again. It might have been pure luck that made me the youngest Sheriff in the state of Iowa, but I'll keep fightin' to prove I'm worthy of the title. "Everyone knows you have a big mouth. You might want to be careful what you say, Shawn. You're the law now." If I didn't know better, I'd say he's thumbin' his nose at me.

"I know what I know about Marlena. You need to take off the rose-colored glasses so you can see what everyone else already does. She's nothing more than a liar and a thief. She's practically a prostitute."

His words punch me in the gut. They feel like a knife that just keeps on twistin', because it has me doubtin' my judgment and what I know to be true about the one girl I can't let go.

My clenched fists stay at my sides. Just barely. "Marlena O'Reilly was hard from the inside out. Love was a sport for her. She shoulda wore a belt, because she held her own. She was a prize-fighter. Whether you knew her for five minutes in the dark, chased her for days, or suffered her blows for weeks or months, eventually she delivered the knock-out blow, and a guy never saw it comin'. Knowin' that, we still stepped into the ring. Marlena was a cold-hearted champion, but that didn't stop too many fools from tryin' to own her," I accuse as I stare him down.

His pale face is a little pink. If I didn't know better, I'd say I got under his skin. "Sounds like you've been sittin' on the Preacher's steps a little too long, Sheriff. That was some sermon you just gave me about a girl you hardly knew."

"All I'm sayin' is, if she'd have been a man, they would have called her a plumber, because she laid a lot of pipe. But double standards are hard to let go of. If she were a guy in high school, she would have been respected, and you know that."

He shakes his head. "I can't believe you're defending a girl who has been with so many guys."

"You're just mad because she wouldn't get with you," I answer.

He rolls his eyes at my words, but there's no denyin' the truth written all over his face. "I never said I wanted to be with her."

"You didn't have to," I taunt at his retreatin' form.

"Think what you want, Sheriff," he yells from across the room, showin' his fiery temper that matches his red hair. "We all know what she was. She made no secrets about her conquests."

"So she kept a little black book. That's not against the law," I say, "but gettin'…" I stop talkin' before the last words escapes me, even though it's barely above a whisper. I can't believe I almost gave her up. I almost forgot I'm the only one in this town who knows about Marlena's daughter. The negative reactions Meagan's been gettin' about her supposed disappearance suggest otherwise.

Meagan's little disappearin' act has me worried, but it also makes me wonder if the apple didn't fall far from the tree. Marlena left town on graduation day, and she never looked back, until things she saw that she shouldn't have seen caught up with her.

I slide the paper back enough to see Marlena's name. Am I lookin' for a missin' girl or an apology that's twelve years too late and as unobtainable as it was the mornin' after the one and only high school dance I attended from the parkin' lot where I laid in the back of a pick-up truck starin' up at the sky, hidin' from my mother, and the rest of my classmates? I wasn't about to go inside and watch Marlena dance all night with a guy who wasn't me.

8

DAY THREE

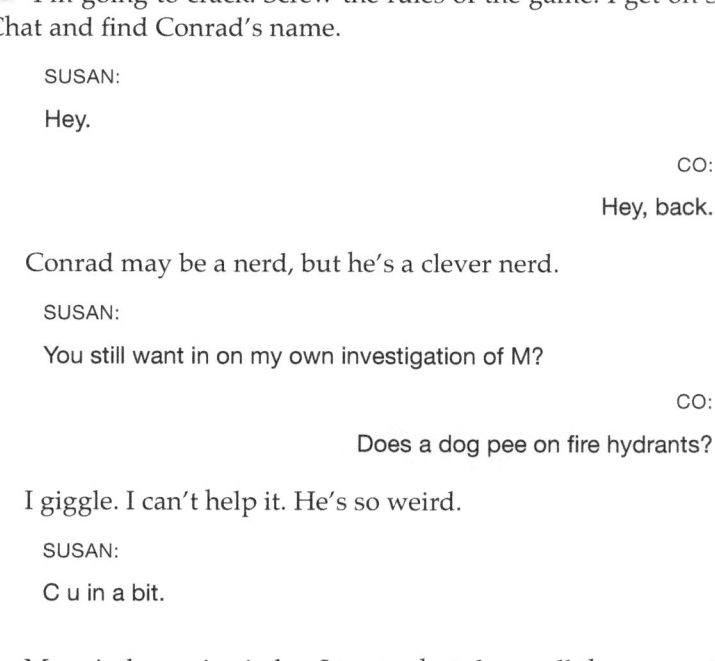

I lay back on my bed and stare up at the ceiling. I know what I'm inviting in, but I have no choice. I can't do this alone, or I'm going to crack. Screw the rules of the game. I get on Snap-Chat and find Conrad's name.

SUSAN:

Hey.

CO:

Hey, back.

Conrad may be a nerd, but he's a clever nerd.

SUSAN:

You still want in on my own investigation of M?

CO:

Does a dog pee on fire hydrants?

I giggle. I can't help it. He's so weird.

SUSAN:

C u in a bit.

My mind runs in circles. I try to shut down all the memories of

Meagan, but I can't. Her words chase themselves around inside my brain as I wander aimlessly around my room picking up. What was she trying to tell me that I wasn't hearing because I stopped listening because she became too much? Do I really want to get the first boy I ever kissed involved in the trouble I'm in? I flop back on my bed and stare up at the motionless ceiling fan, one more thing that hasn't moved since Meagan left. She loved the fan on. I hate it. It made me cold, and I can't take things blowing in my ear. It was easier to wear thicker socks, sweatpants, and hoodies to bed than fight with her. I rest my hands on my chest as I lay half on and half off my bed.

Footsteps pound up my stairs. My bedroom door flies open. "Hey, Conrad," I manage as I half-slide off my bed so I can stand. "Thanks for coming over."

He grins at me from behind his glasses. His wavy brown hair flirts with his eyebrows. An easy grin pops out. "That's no problem. You know I love a good mystery. And it's Co, by the way."

"Co like the co-op?" I tease.

"I go by Co because Conrad was my grand-ather's name. I'm hardly an old man," he jokes in a manner worthy of a sixty-year-old man, but I'm not about to correct him.

"Right. Sorry."

He reaches over and shuts the door from the spot he plopped down on my floor. "First things first, we have to have a cover story," he says.

"What do you mean?"

He rolls his eyes and leans back on his palms. "I mean, we can't tell them what we're really doing, trying to solve a crime, so we have to come up with a reason that I'm here," he explains.

I think I know who's he's talking about, but it's hard to say with Conrad. "Who are they?" I whisper all secretive.

He stares at me like he can't believe what I just asked. "The parental units," he states.

"Oh. Right. We could say we're working on a science project," I say.

He shakes his head back and forth. "We all know that's not true. You're not a science person."

He's right, but I didn't think he knew that about me. We haven't talked since I was twelve and he was eleven, and I kissed him at his brother Padrick's birthday party. "How did you get here?" I ask out of curiosity.

"I rode my bike," he explains.

"That's like eight miles from here," I say.

"It's six and a half. I know a shortcut. Why does it matter? I'm here now. Let's get to work," he insists.

"On what?" I ask.

"On figuring out where Meagan is," he says before he stops short. "You wanted me to come over to help you find her, right? Because if you don't want my services, just say so, and I'll leave, but there will be a fifteen-dollar cancellation fee."

I'm so confused. "What?"

He digs a black card from his pocket and hands it to me. "You're operating as a private investigator," I say.

"Junior, PI," he corrects.

"But you're fourteen-years-old," I insist.

He clears his throat and looks a little sheepish, but I sense a hint of irritation. "I'm almost fifteen, but whatever. There are some advantages to being young and clueless. It's the perfect age if you think about it. I'm young enough no one suspects I'm doing anything questionable. They will underestimate my ability to notice anything out of the ordinary. It allows me to go where I need to without arousing suspicion."

His answer actually makes a lot of sense, but his positive attitude lacks the cynicism and intentional tone that Meagan's always had. "That's why you Snapped me, because you know I'm in trouble."

He shrugs his shoulders. "I heard they took you downtown. I know who Meagan is. I heard she's missing. I heard you might be in trouble. If we can find Meagan, you won't be in trouble." He snaps his fingers. "And I like a good mystery. This will definitely put my sleuthing skills to the test." I admire his confidence, but I'm doubtful of what a fourteen-year-old boy can discover.

"And you have no choice. You can't hire a real PI because you're fifteen. I'm guessing you know things you don't want to tell the police, and I'm guessing there might be someone coming after you," he adds before raising a finger. "*Or* this might just be an amped-up game of Crack-It, because Meagan is sick and twisted. Either way, I want in."

My ears burn. I can't believe she told him. Crack-It was our game. She's the one who insisted it was just between us. "How do you know about Crack-It?" I ask.

"She told me," he answers.

"When?" I ask. I feel so betrayed.

He looks a little caught. "Um, when she found out I like to solve puzzles and things. She got me all excited about the game right before she told me it was a members only game, and I wasn't a member," he says, and his voice is quieter. Now that I can believe.

"I'm sorry, Co. I had no idea," I answer.

He ducks his head. "I figured you didn't."

I throw a scrunchie at him. "Are you sure you want to find her?"

He laughs a little, and I feel less bad that she hurt his feelings on purpose. "Yeah. I want to find her. If she's doing all this for the name of the game, that's a really crappy thing to do to a friend. You've never been anything but nice to her."

"Thanks," I say. I feel inadequate. I've done nothing to deserve his kindness.

"Can I see her room?" he asks as we stand up.

His question surprises me. "How do you know this isn't her room?" I ask about the time I wish I hadn't. Something tells me his answer is going to be a bit much.

He blinks. "Because you're in it," he says with a small smile. "And because of your collection of boy band posters," he says as he points at my walls. "Meagan would never put those on her walls. She probably has vintage horror movie posters on her walls."

It's strange how spot-on his answer is. "Sounds like you know us better than most," I offer.

He looks all embarrassed. It's kind of cute. *Wait, what*? "Hel-lo.

They're called eyes," he jokes as he points at his face. "Let's get moving."

I nod. "Sure, but we have to be quiet," I warn him. "I don't think Mom wants me in there. She's trying to keep my dad from getting more upset."

He steps closer to me. His grin hides behind his pointer finger. My stomach feels all jumpy inside. What is going on? I can't like him. I'm a sophomore. He's a ninth grader. It's one more thing Amber and her stupid group of friends would tease me about. He's just so quirky. "I think I'm taller than you," he says.

I take a step back. "Yep," I say as I sneak past him and tiptoe down the hall to the door that leads to the half staircase leading to the strange little room off the attic. We walk down the middle of her room because it's the tallest part. The ceiling is narrow. The walls slant in a downwards fashion on both sides. A single bed is lined up against the far wall. A short but wide bookshelf sits beside it. Her three floor lamps are arranged in a triangular pattern. Two bean bags face each other. I bump into one and put a hand on it to move it.

"Stop," he says in a sharp tone.

I freeze.

"We need to leave everything exactly as it is," he instructs. "We need to know if she was trying to leave us any clues."

"She disappeared," I hiss at him. "She obviously doesn't want to be found."

"Unless she was taken," he says as he sits down on the bean-bag, "against her will."

The thought has occurred to me. More than once. I just don't want to believe it. I sink into the beanbag across from him, lean in, and grab him by the arm. "I need to tell you something," I whisper.

"What?" he asks, but his twinkling eyes are glued to my hand holding onto his arm. I drop his arm.

"She says she's in danger."

His eyes widen. "She talked to you recently? When?"

I close my eyes and try to think, but my thoughts race inside my head. "Like a few days ago," I say.

"Do you think she's in danger?" he asks.

My eyes water. My throat tightens. "I think she could be, yes, but it's better than thinking she's dead." I force myself to keep talking. "I thought she was dead because she let herself be thrown over the bridge and into the water."

To his credit, Conrad listens intently, doesn't look at me like I'm crazy, and he seems genuinely concerned for my safety. "Why would she do that?"

"I haven't figured that part out yet. I mean, she had been playing dead for at least a month. It was a new game she started playing. It was creepy and weird, and she was really good at it," I say.

"Why would she do that?" he asks.

I stomp my foot because he asked the same question twice, and I don't have a straight answer. "I don't know, okay? I mean, I thought she was doing it for attention because I stopped hanging out with her as much because I was hanging out with Ryan."

Co wrinkles his nose. "Ryan, as in Ryan Sams?"

The look on his face has me all defensive. "What's wrong with Ryan? All the girls like him."

He gives me a look. "Don't tell me you don't know he's asked like half the junior high girls for inappropriate pictures."

I gasp. "What? No, no way. He's like sixteen. That's just…"

"Against the law? Disgusting? Predatory?" Conrad rattles off.

My hand flies up. "Okay, okay. I hear you. He didn't ever…" I stop talking. He did. Once. About a week after we were officially dating, kind of. I don't know. I suck at being a high-school girl *in like*. He Snapped me at like 1:00a.m. I was asleep. The next morning, I got a Snap from him. He was all *why'd you send me a picture of a naked Barbie doll?*

As soon as he said it, I knew what happened and who did it. Meagan sent the Barbie pictures, because she doesn't take any shit from anyone, not even the most popular boy in school. I was mad at her for interfering with our relationship, but I was even more mad at him for asking for what he asked for in the first place. "I'm no one's 1 a.m. pin-up girl," I had Snapped back. I didn't hear from him for two days, and I was sure we were over. But then he showed up at my door with flowers, and I forgave him. We went out for a pizza. It was such a fun night, until I got home to find Meagan sitting in my room with an accusatory look on her face.

"I can't believe you went out with him again. He's such a jerk," she said.

"He told me it was a test, and I passed," I argued, even though I knew my answer was weak.

"Yeah. That's just what guys say when they know they messed up because they're pervs," she had all but shouted in my face.

"You're jealous because you don't have a boyfriend," I yelled back.

She laughed in my face. It hurt more than I'd like to admit. "What are you talking about? You don't have one either," she'd snarled.

"Susan?" Conrad's voice reorients me to the present.

"I'm sorry, what," I answer.

"Did she have any sort of diary? Some place she wrote things down?"

I remember the torn pages she left for me to find. I should tell him, but I'm not ready to share it.

"She liked to draw," I offered.

"Oils? Paints? What sort of drawing?" Co asks.

"More like charcoal on paper," I answer.

"So, we are looking for a sketch pad," he says.

"I think so," I agree.

He's down on his hands and knees. He lifts her mattress.

"What are you doing?" I ask.

"People rarely leave things they want hidden in plain sight," he mutters. "Get your phone light over here," he grunts.

I duck down right before I hit my head on her low ceiling. I see nothing, but something hits the wall. He drops the mattress. He must've heard it too. I dig around and find a sketch pad sticking out the side of her pillowcase. I hand it to him. He flips through it. "That's weird. They're all like curved lines and shading."

I flip clean to the back of the tablet. "It's a shallot or an onion," I announce.

He looks confused. "What does that mean? Why would she repeatedly draw the same thing over and over?"

I keep the sketchpad close to my chest and flop on the beanbag. "I'm the shallot. She's the onion."

His confusion remains in place. "I don't get it."

"I'm an imitation," I say. "That's what she said," I explain.

"An imitation of what?" he asks, as if I said the dumbest thing ever.

"An imitation of her," I explain.

He stares at me like I'm crazy. "No, you're not. You don't hurt people on purpose. You don't play games with people's feelings. You don't try to control other people with emotional blackmail."

I flinch at his harsh words. "Emotional blackmail? What does that mean?"

He looks away from me. "Telling people you're going to do something bad because you're so sad," he says.

"You don't think she meant it?" I argue. "We were all there. She was on the bridge. She would have jumped if someone hadn't grabbed a hold of her," I say and tear up again at the memory. She was only thirteen years old. Maybe she's been trying to tell me something for a long time. I just haven't been listening.

"She didn't come down until Tonya took her hand," he says. "Don't you remember?"

I shake my head. "Remember what?"

"Three other people offered their hands to Meagan. She refused. She called Tonya's name over and over. She *forced* Tonya to help her. I think Meagan thought her little stunt would make her popular," he explains.

"No," I say, "that's not how it happened."

"Yes, it is. I was there too," he says in a quiet voice while he circles the room lifting things with a pencil.

I stifle a giggle. He looks like a detective on TV

"What? What's so funny?" he demands.

"Where's your latex gloves?" I tease.

He reaches in his pocket. I cringe a little. "If you insist," he says with a grin as he shoves his hand into one before putting on the other one. Co opens every dresser drawer. He goes through them

65

in a quick but thorough manner. He even gets on his knees and looks at the underside before leaning over to peek underneath the dresser. Satisfied, he moves on to her closet. His hands rifle through every pocket of every item of clothing. He turns to face me. "Look closely. Do you see anything that is out of place? Is there anything missing?" he asks.

I think. "Her small purse is missing, but that would make sense because she took it everywhere."

"Is that all?" he asks.

I stare at the closet bulb just above his head. "Is there some-thing in there?" I ask as I point at the shelves.

He turns and looks up. "This could be a clue," he says with excitement in his tone, and then it hits me.

"Her Crack-It box," I say.

"What about it?" he asks.

"Her Crack-It box is missing. She had one and I had one. We kept them on our top shelves. Hers is gone," I answer.

He puts the bulb back in place. "Where is yours?"

I frown. "It's in my room."

"Are you sure?" he asks as his hand goes in his pocket. What is he hiding, and why?

I turn off the lights. "Let's go see."

We tiptoe back down the steps and return to my room. Mom pops her head in. "Hey, there. What're we doing?"

"Forensics practice," I announce way too loudly. I point at Conrad. "Mom, you remember Conrad? He goes by Co now."

She stares at the two of us. "Aren't you in eighth grade?"

"No. I'm a freshman," he answers.

"How nice for you," she comments in her mom-like way.

"We're considering doing something together," I supply. "We're trying something new."

Mom continues to stare at me. "I didn't know you were in forensics," she says.

"You told me to try new things," I answer. "So I am," I say as I force myself not to shout. "Can we please practice in private?" I ask before shutting the door.

"You need to chill," Co suggests.

I give him a shove. "My *best friend* is missing. I just found out she's most likely alive when I thought she wasn't. Don't tell me to calm down," I whisper shout.

He steps up in my space and stares me down. My stomach has serious butterflies. I try to shut them down. I am not about to be crushing on a ninth-grade boy in the middle of my personal crisis. "Hey," he says.

"What?" I answer back with the same amount of hostility I had two seconds ago while I was lecturing him.

"I understand that you are upset and worried for Meagan, but this is not the time for a full-on meltdown. Get it together, or I'm out of here," he threatens. "You owe me twenty-five dollars."

What is going on? "I never agreed to pay you anything," I say. His eyes widen. He holds up a gloved hand and proceeds to start peeling it off. "Stop," I say. "I'm calm," I promise as I will myself to stop shaking from the inside out. "I can be calm," I say again, like a mantra. I feel his unwavering stare. It's unnerving. "Stop staring," I whisper.

He turns away from me. "I wasn't. Okay, I was, but not for the reasons you think I was," he adds, reminding me why I almost didn't tell him to come over. Sometimes he's too honest. "What are we doing in forensics?" he asks in a hopeful tone.

I'm so lost right now. "What?"

"Forensics," he says again. "What are we practicing?"

This boy makes my head hurt. "I'm not in forensics," I say "It's our cover, remember? It was your brilliant idea."

"Yeah, I know," he says. "But I think you should join. Paddy and I are both in forensics. We really like it."

I do a giant eye roll. "Of course, you and your brother are in forensics. You're both naturals on stage." I turn back to him. "I am not."

"I don't know about that," he argues. "That lie you just told your mom was pretty convincing."

His statement has too much truth. It makes me feel bad. "That's different. I told her that because I had to."

"No, you didn't. You chose to," he corrects me.

"Co," I say, getting in his face again. "Don't be such a choir boy," I tease, even though I feel mean. I'm the one who should feel bad, not him. I tell myself I'm standing so close to him because we are whispering so my mother won't hear what we are saying.

"I'm not in the choir. I don't like to sing," he says. "But I won't lie to your mother, so I'm telling Paddy you're joining forensics," he says as he takes off a glove and starts texting away. "He'll get you on the team," he announces in a way that suggests it's my life-long dream to perform in a front of judges and have them critique my inability to be much braver than I am.

"Whatever," I grump. "What am I supposed to be looking for?"

"The box," he says in an exasperated tone.

"What?" I ask.

"The Crack-It box. Where is it? That's what we came in here to find."

I stumble past him and get down on my hands and knees to crawl into the corner of my closet. My hands fumble around in the dark, but I recognize its shape. I hold it out to him. "Here you go," I say.

I hear the lid hit the floor. His gloved hands rustle around. "This isn't yours," he says.

"What?" I ask as I get back on my feet.

"This box isn't yours," he states.

"How do you know that?"

"Um, because it says, 'this box belongs to Meagan Davis so keep your thievin' hands to yourself.'"

I giggle at his words. "I remember when she wrote that. We were sitting in here on the floor. It was time for bed. We'd already been given two warnings, but Meagan wanted for five more minutes." I rock back on my heels and cross my arms across my chest. "She always wanted five more minutes," I say more to myself than Co. I look off to the side. "We had bunkbeds, but it was ridiculous. She never slept in her own bed. She always crawled into mine," I say, and then I stop talking.

"Do you know why you have her box?" he asks.

I shake my head back and forth. "No. I mean, I didn't take it." My eyes meet his again. "I never took anything of hers. She was very possessive of her stuff. I don't know if it's because she lost her mom, or what," I say, because I feel like I'm betraying her trust.

"What do you mean?" he asks.

"Well, like we were best friends, okay, but one time I was mad at her, and I knew how she felt about her clothes, so I went into her closet and took something she never wore, and I wore it." I take a deep breath. "The whole thing was so dumb. We'd been fighting over a boy who didn't know either of us existed, but that's beside the point. She took a picture of me with my phone when I was sleeping, like the heavy sleep where you wake up and you've got drool or whatever, and she sent it to him with some stupid caption about me drooling over him." My face flames even now at the admission. I wave my hands as if to erase it. "I was angry with her, okay. So I took this hoodie of hers that she swore was so hideous she wouldn't be caught dead in it, and I wore it."

"What happened?" he asks.

"Well, that was like the second day that she refused to ride to school with me because we were in a fight, like the first and only fight we've ever had that was seriously bad. I mean, we'd had fights before but not like this," I say as my throat tightens. I can't believe I forgot how mad she got over a stupid shirt. "So I show up to school in her shirt and she's waiting by the front door, acting like she's not waiting, but she totally was. It's like she wanted me to see her there, while not acting like she wanted me to see her."

"What did she do?" Co says in a voice that tells me he wants me to hurry up and finish the story.

"I saw her. She looked at the shirt, made some strange face, and then walked right past me to the parking lot." I stare at him. "She just left school. She was gone all day, and I was like trying not to panic because I knew my parents would be getting a call, and Mom would show up at school like she always did when Meagan got into some sort of trouble, and then Dad would be mad when he got home because we all had to deal with Meagan's drama as usual, and he didn't sign up for any of it," I say, and then feel weird that I'm spilling all my family secrets to Conrad.

"It's okay. Anything you say to me while on the job is strictly confidential," he assures me, and I tell myself not to feel so bad for spilling all that to a fourteen-year-old boy, because he's not like any fourteen-year-old boy I ever knew.

"I went through the whole school day unable to focus on anything because Meagan is so overly dramatic. I had no idea what she was doing. I wanted to text her to tell her I was sorry, but I couldn't do it, because I wasn't, because she made me so mad. And it was just a stupid shirt. She was overreacting. What she did to me was way worse. She sent some super embarrassing picture to my first-ever crush. She had no right," I say, getting all fired up again.

"What did she do?" Co asks for the third time.

"The whole day went by, and it was terrible. I couldn't pay attention in any class. The only thing that made it a little better was Ryan stopped me in the hall and asked me out. That was so cool." I say, and, for half a second, I forget that I'm mad at Ryan for breaking up with me.

"Su-san. Fo-cus," Co says.

"I came home, and she had moved out of our room," I say in a flat voice. "We shared a room for four years. I wore her shirt one time without her permission, and she moved out."

Co blinks a few times. He studies me as if he's trying to decide if I'm exaggerating the truth or omitting some important fact. "That's straight up sociopathic," he says.

I open my mouth to defend her and close it again. "I shouldn't have told you any of that," I say instead. "It's just, since all of this started and everything has happened, I keep going over her words and actions, trying to figure out what I missed that she was trying to tell me," I say, as I try to get him to understand. "What if she was trying to tell me she was in trouble, but I wasn't hearing her because we were fighting? Or what if she was trying to push me away because she knew she was in danger and she didn't want me to get hurt?"

Co laughs out loud. "Don't kid yourself. That girl doesn't look out for anyone but herself. She wasn't worried about putting anyone else in danger," he states.

I take a deep breath. "A good detective has to be objective,

Con-." I stop midword. It's so awkward. "I mean, Co. You can't let your opinion of my friend cloud your judgment."

He slaps his hand on his thigh. "She's not your friend, Susan. Meagan is an instigator and an isolator. She pushed everyone away from you."

His words sound so angry. I had no idea Conrad saw all that. If he saw it, and he's not even that close to me at school, what does that mean? Have I been so closed off that I didn't see everyone talking about us? Am I that self-involved? I don't know what to say. I wish he would stop staring. "What?" I say in a small voice which reminds me of too many conversations I had with Meagan.

He steps into my closet, still staring. It's so strange. I turn away to scan the shelves, but mostly to stop looking at him. We stand back-to-back. "What are you doing?" I ask as his back bumps into mine.

"Looking for clues." My underwear on top of my dirty clothes hamper catches the corner of my eye. He stands beside it. All I see is his hand almost bumping the plastic corner of my hamper. It's too weird. I rip a hoodie off a hanger and toss it on top of the hamper. "What are you doing," he asks me.

"Covering up my dirty clothes," I say.

"Why?" he asks. If he were any other guy, I would think he was being a turd to embarrass me, but he's not. He's Co.

"I don't want you to see my…" I stop talking and look him in the eye to gage his reaction. He seriously has no clue. "I don't want you to see my underwear," I get out before turning away from him to look somewhere else, anywhere but at him. Why can't I keep my awkward mouth shut?

"Everybody wears them," he offers. I say nothing in response.

9

"Tell me about your trip downtown," Co comments as we go over every single item on the shelves, of which there are many. I can't believe I'm letting him go through my stuff like this. She'd be mad enough to murder me if she knew I was involving him. It's breaking the rules, but I don't care. Meagan is missing. There was a gun. This isn't just Crack-It anymore.

I can't ask Mom and Dad for help. They're too busy trying to keep me out of trouble. I get it, but she's my friend, and no one is looking for her. Except for the man with the gun. If she's still alive, but she's with him, what can that mean?

"I already told you," I say in exasperation.

"Well, tell me again. There must be a clue there somewhere."

My head hurts. I'm hungry. "Give me a minute, Co. Please."

"Okay, fine. If you don't want to talk about that, tell me why you kissed me."

My face flushes. I can't believe he just asked me that. "We were kids, Co. It didn't mean anything," I say, about the time I feel him tense up behind me. "I'm so sorry. That was such a Meagan thing to say," I offer.

He laughs a little, but it doesn't sound sincere. "Yeah, it was." He clears his throat. Great. More awkwardness is coming. "If it didn't mean anything to you, why did you do it?"

That's a fair question. Conrad has never been anything but truthful. I flinch when I realize sometimes I'd almost rather he lie to me. Maybe I've been friends with Meagan for too long. "I guess I wanted to know what it would be like to kiss somebody famous," I tease.

His eyes sparkle and shine. A grin sneaks out, lighting up his face. Whoa. There's something about him that totally snuck up on me. I feel all warm inside. What's going on?

"Okay," he says before turning back around to grab something off the top shelf. "I remember this hoodie. You wore it like every day."

I smile as I trace the white heart on the black hoodie. "Mom bought me that. She was so in love with it. I don't know why. It wasn't like Mom to get excited about clothes, but for some reason, she loved that shirt." I pause. "But I wore this in ninth grade. We weren't in the same school then."

He turns around to put it back. "I, uh, I would ride my bike to the bus stop to see you get on the bus in the mornings."

My heart skips a beat at the thought of him riding six miles out of the way just to see me. "You did?"

"Yep. What can I say? I was kind of a stalker."

I giggle. "I think it's kind of sweet." I lay a hand on his arm. "I'm sorry I didn't see you."

He shrugs me off. "Yeah, well. I guess our kiss meant more to me than it did to you."

His words aren't cutting or bitter. If anything, he sounds a little hurt. "I didn't mean to cause you pain, Co. I guess I was just a little bit of a weird-o."

His laughter eases my embarrassment. "Gee, thanks. First you tell me our kiss didn't mean anything, and now you're telling me you're strange for kissing me at all."

I close my eyes. "Co, for being a PI, you don't read a room very well. What I'm trying to say is that I was a strange girl for kissing you out of the blue with no pretense. The reason I kissed you was odd. I didn't kiss you because I liked you, I kissed you because..." I stop talking and open my eyes to look at him. I'm only making it worse. "This is not at all what I was trying to say."

He's smirking, which is a little sexy, but mostly a relief to me. At least he's not looking more upset. I wish I could hit the rewind button on the entire conversation. "How about we make it even?"

"Excuse me?"

He steps closer and leans in. His chin bumps mine. He sighs and starts to back away. "I can't even get that…"

My hand flies to the back of his neck. I can't take how I made him feel. "You're overthinking it, Co," I murmur right before my lips touch his. Our kiss is slow and hesitant. It feels a little weird. It's like we're both distracted or something. I feel terrible because my mind races. It's definitely not the same as kissing Ryan. Ryan is taller, and more hands on. I could tell Ryan had kissed a lot of girls. And that fact made me feel insecure. I feel uncertain now, but it's a whole different kind of uncertainty.

I'm trying to shut my mind down or at least stop thinking about Ryan when I'm kissing Conrad. His hands are on my shoulders, gripping, but he's pushing me away.

"That's it, Susan." He stopped kissing me. Why is he so excited about it?

"What?"

"We're both overthinking."

That's it, Susan." He stopped kissing me. Why is he so excited about it?

"What?"

"We're both overthinking."

He stares at me with such expectation. This is so peculiar. There's no way he knew I was thinking about Ryan,

is there? "I'm trying not to. I'm sorry."

"Why be sorry? We just have to change our approach."

Now I'm really confused. What other approach is there to kissing a boy? Attraction is all about chemistry, not

science.

"Excuse me?"

"Mea-gan. Let's try simplicity."

Oh. Duh. "Yeah, Meagan," I say, but my mind is somewhere else.

He steps out of the closet. He paces the room. His hands slap his legs in a rhythmic way. He stops mid-step and looks at me. "Oh. You thought I was talking about our…"

"What just happened?" I ask, cutting him off. I don't want to talk about the kiss anymore. It obviously meant nothing to him if all he can think about is the investigation. Which is what I should be thinking about, and not comparing kissing Ryan to kissing Conrad, when Conrad didn't even make a move on me. Well, he kind of did, but that's because I sort of dared him to. I don't know. Ugh. I have to stop thinking about something that's not there and isn't important.

"Susan."

"Yeah."

"Simplify."

"Got it."

He crosses his arms on his chest. "You need to start talking, because I know there are things you're thinking that you're not saying. But if we're going to work as a team, you have to tell me."

I sit down on the floor, crisscross applesauce like we used to do in elementary school. "Fine," I say as I stare at the rug. "If she's with this guy who had the gun and she's still alive, that would mean he needs something from her, right?"

"Or they're in it together," he answers.

"Yeah, but if they were, wouldn't they be asking for something by now?"

"From whom?"

I feel like I'm hitting a brick wall. "I don't know."

"He can't be holding her for ransom because you said she has no family. That's how she ended up in foster care."

I nod my head. "Yeah."

"Well, now she's been missing for forty-eight hours."

His statement confuses me. "So?" I answer.

"That's how long it has to be before she's considered a missing person, and so I guess she's officially a missing person now."

How could I forget that?

"But, if they're thinking she's a runaway, then the search for her might not get top priority."

"Yeah. Because she's sixteen. That makes a difference," he confirms.

"Except she's not."

He snorts. "Obviously she's not a priority. She's pulled this crap before. We already said that."

"She's not sixteen," I say.

"Oh. She's seventeen?"

"No. She's fifteen. Like me."

"Then technically she's a missing person."

This is so maddening. I feel like I'm talking in circles and not getting anywhere. "The cop said I was the last person to see her alive. He made me feel like I was a suspect."

"All they found was her phone, right?"

"Yeah."

He's quiet for too many seconds. I want to tell him the rest, but how can I? There's no way to explain how I threw a body off a bridge without sounding like a terrible person.

"Co."

"Yeah?" I don't want to ask, but I have to. I'm tired of feeling like I'm completely insane. "It has to be her texting me, right? I mean, another person wouldn't text me and pose as her if they're not asking me for anything. What would they have to gain?"

"That's a good question."

"I can't believe she would run off like this and involve a man with a gun to win some stupid game she started when we were kids. I can't. She *has* to be in some sort of trouble."

He clears his throat. "Maybe she tried to take the game to the next level, and she got in over her head."

"Maybe."

An alarm sounds on his phone. "I'm sorry. I gotta go."

"Got another PI appointment? You're busy," I tease.

He stands over me. Something feels different between us. He's not as nervous as he was when he got here. He nudges my foot with his. "So far, you're my only my client. When this is over, I expect good reviews."

What happened to his voice, and when did Conrad learn how

to flirt? I should stand up. It feels weird looking up at him. I dig into his toe through the end of his shoe with my finger, pushing as hard as I can. "We have to solve the case first."

"Don't worry. I will." His foot bumps mine again.

Why is he still standing here? I look up at him. "Is there something else?" "Let me know if you hear from her," he orders, as if he's a cop.

I nod my head. "I will."

He walks across the room with a little swagger if I'm not mistaken. Just before he goes out, he turns around to look at me one more time. "For the record, I've never kissed a criminal. You're my first."

All I can do is smile as he turns and walks out. Conrad Barnes is more complex than I gave him credit for.

10

Badge 343

hawn's comment about Marlena and Hamilton "Hammy" Harris won't go away. He hit his head fallin' off some scaffolding he was crawlin' around on in the dark. Everyone knows that. He's the one who said it when they found him wanderin' down a dirt road. My head hurts tryin' to remember Hamilton from our high-school days. He wasn't into sports. He wasn't exactly the academic type. He mostly hung out in the shop.

Against my better judgment, I head to the front of the buildin'. It's almost five o'clock. Maybe Laurel has forgotten about bein' pissed at me earlier today. I scan the empty room. "Dang it," I mutter.

She pops up from somewhere on the floor. "Hey. I was lookin' for the back of my earring."

I mosey over to her desk to talk to the back of her. She's still on her knees. "Do you remember Hamilton Harris?"

She turns back to look at me. "Maybe. Why?"

"What kind of guy was he?"

"I don't know. He was a bit of a lurker. I mean he liked to stare at us girls, but he never did more than that."

I wish I could let this go. She's probably gonna say what Shawn already said. "Do you remember hearin' anythin' about him and Marlena?"

She whips back around. Her hands go over the thin carpet in a bit of a hurry, considerin' she's lookin' for a microscopic piece of metal. "Well, he used to follow her around. Like in his car. She said something about it once, but she was mostly making fun."

"Did she seem afraid?"

She laughs. "Marlena wasn't afraid of anything. You know that. Anyway, I guess his persistence paid off, 'cause I heard they hooked up or whatever."

"And that's all?" I ask. I don't believe a word of it. Marlena wouldn't give Hamilton the time of day just because he stalked her. Would she?

She sits up, places her hands on her knees and turns back to look at me again. "No. I heard she tried to kill him."

I laugh a little. "What, like she's some sort of prayin' mantis or somethin'?"

Laurel's face is confused. It's almost cute. She's not a bad-lookin' woman. She just doesn't do it for me. I wish Shawn hadn't said anythin' about her crush, but that was years ago. It has nothin' to do with what's goin' on right now. "Say what?"

"After prayin' mantis mate, the female often eats the male. She starts by chewin' off his head."

Her nose wrinkles. "That's disgusting."

"Yep."

"Did you believe it?"

Her eyes widen. "If you said it, I imagine it's true."

My face heats. Her blind confidence in me is flatterin', but it scares me. I can't get an over-inflated head. If I do that, I won't think straight. "I meant about Marlena and Hamilton," I say in a quieter voice.

"Oh."

I know this is the last thing she wants to talk about, Marlena's love life, but I have to know more about that night. I tap my foot. "I'm just tryin' to figure out why if it was such a wide-spread rumor, no one ever told me."

She sniffs. "Because they knew you wouldn't listen."

"Because I don't like gossip," I reply.

She rolls her eyes. "Because it had to do with *her.*"

"So you think she tried to kill Hamilton after she slept with him. What sense would that make?"

She shrugs. "Nothing that girl did made sense."

"Maybe not to us," I muse. "I just find it very hard to believe she would willingly try to kill someone. She wasn't the type of girl to lose her head over a guy," I argue.

Laurel looks defeated and surprised at the same time. "I never thought about it like that," she admits.

I hate how good I feel about being right. "It's my job to be analytical," I reason.

"Yeah, well. It's hard to be objective when it comes to Marlena."

"Why did you hate her?"

Laurel's eyes drop to the floor. "I didn't hate her." She takes a deep breath. "Okay, maybe I did. A little. But you know, it's just because she was nothing, okay. Call me a snob if you want, but we all knew where she lived. In a little shack down a dirt road in the middle of nowhere. The only time guys drove down that road to see her was after dark. They went so far as to turn off their head-lights. That's how badly they didn't want to be seen at her place." She laughs, but it's bitter. "Any guy who had half a brain knew they better not go out there without a spare, because they were bound to get a flat tire."

"Made for good business at the local gas station," I joke, and immediately feel bad. "They sold a lot of tires."

"And she knew it," she continues, as if I didn't say anything. "She knew how the girls at school felt about her. It's like it fueled her fire. She went out of her way to go after other girls' boyfriends."

Her words hurt because they're absolutely true. "Guess I shoulda had a girlfriend," I answer. "Then maybe she woulda looked at me."

Laurel kicks my ankle, surprisin' me. "You had plenty of girls lookin' at you, Sheriff. You won't be gettin' any sympathy from me. You just didn't see any of them 'cause you were too busy lookin' at her."

"Well. I can't argue that," I say as I lean over and pick up the tiny back on the other side of her desk. I hold it out as some sort of peace offering. "Here."

She takes it from my hand. "Thanks. I never would have found it. I was looking in the wrong place."

Her statement is like a smack in the face. "Exactly," I say.

"I can see you're onto something. I'm glad I could help."

I nod my head in answer. "For the record, Laurel, I don't blame you for bein' so narrow-minded. It was the popular opinion. But I can't blame her either. She shouldn't have been chasin' other girls' boyfriends, but that's not why she didn't have friends. Marlena was a lot of things, but stupid wasn't one of them. It wouldn't have mattered how nice she was. All anyone here saw once they knew her was her last name and the house she lived in, just like you said. Even if she tried to forget her last name, no one else would."

"Maybe, but she didn't even try."

"Would you have tried?" I ask, even though I'm pretty sure our conversation about Marlena is over in more ways than one.

"It's been a long day, Sheriff. I'll see you tomorrow." Laurel's words are short and clipped. It's just as well. There's somewhere else I need to be.

It's fifteen miles out of the way, but I'm not pullin' up there in a squad car. I hop in my 1985 Ford pick-up, toss my badge in the glovebox, remove my waist holster, and shove my other gun in my ankle strap. Too soon I'm at the one place I swore I'd never set foot in again after my father dragged me out the first time. The door swings open right as I'm grabbin' the doorknob.

I step inside about the time I remember I didn't exchange hats. Shit. Half of me wants to duck and cover and go back to the truck. The other half is committed. Judgin' by the hush which just came over the room, I've already been spotted. I head for the bar. Disappointment fills me when I notice the one guy I'm lookin' for, the guy who's always here like clockwork, is nowhere to be seen. First my hat, and now no guy. That's two strikes.

I sit down on a stool at the far end and prop my foot on the bottom of the stool next to me. A guy sittin' at a table raises an eyebrow. "You can't wear that in here," he says as he points lazily at my ankle.

"It's a conceal-and-carry state, and you know that," I answer in the most non-confrontational way possible.

"Give 'em a Shirley Temple," the guy says with a smirk on his face.

I'm pissed, but I'm not about to let him see he's gettin' under my skin. "Sounds good to me. You buyin'?"

He gets up out of his chair. He's a bear of a man. He's gotta be a Garrett. They're all the same. Barrel chests, big mouths, and empty heads. At least that's what my dad always said. He slaps a twenty down on the bar before turnin' to lean into my face. It takes all I've got not to cower. "Get what yer after and then get outta here. The law don't go around here."

The bartender sets a drink in front of me with a strange look on his face. "One Shirley Temple."

I raise the glass in the bear's face, tauntin' him. Dad might be dragggin' my stupid butt outta here again. "Thanks for the drink, but you're not my type," I say with a wink.

His meaty fist catches me right in the eye. I knew it was comin' and I didn't duck. I don't know how I'm still on my stool, or why he's just standin' here, starin'. I catch movement behind him.

Gary slaps a bag of peas on the bar. "Put this on your face." He shoves the other guy in the arm. "Go sit down. Show's over."

The man won't stop starin'. "It's not over until I say it's over."

"Go sit down if you ever want another beer in my bar," Gary orders.

I hold the frozen peas on my face. "The next bar's about twenty-five miles in any direction," I mumble.

"What're you sayin'?"

"I'm sayin' that's a lot of DUI's you'll be rackin' up in the name of stupidity and stubbornness," I argue as I turn to face him head on, in case he decides to punch me again.

"You gonna slap me with an assault charge?" he asks, but he doesn't sound too worried.

"Nah. I figure havin' to work will irritate you more than layin' around in a prison cell for a month or two eatin' free meals and watchin' TV," I challenge.

"Okay, then," he says before goin' back to his table.

I look over at Gary. "Got a minute?"

He drops the towel he was about to throw over his shoulder. "Do I have a choice?" he asks as he gestures for me to follow him.

His brightly colored office with all its pastels is a stark contrast to the dimly lit bar. "Love what you've done with the place," I say as I take in the multiple pictures of fully-clothed women drawn in abstract ways. The most obvious part of each picture are their eyes.

"Thanks. I like to think they're all watching me," he jokes. It's nice to know some things haven't changed.

I sit down in the chair across from where he sits behind his desk piled high with papers and ledgers. "How long you been runnin' this place?"

"About six years."

"I hear you bought it off of Charley Pierce before he ran it into the ground."

He does a desk tap with his hands. "Yeah, well. It was good timing. I was debating between working construction for my dad or I didn't know what, and then the bar was up for sale. I went for it."

"Looks like you're doin' alright," I offer.

"Stayin' in the black, anyway," he agrees.

"I'm not gonna beat around the bush, Gary. I heard a rumor today, and I gotta ask you somethin'."

He looks a little sick. I think he knows. "Okay."

"It's about Hamilton."

His face tightens. "What about him?"

"Did he have a thing for Marlena?"

His eyes dart to the side. "I'm four years younger than him. You know that, right?"

I nod. "Yep."

"I wasn't in high school with him."

"Okay."

"Whatever happened with him and girls, I didn't have a clue."

I want to believe him, but he sounds a little too desperate to be tellin' me the whole truth. "You never heard anything about your brother and Marlena?" I ask again.

He stands up and starts pacin'. "Look. I run a bar, okay. I'm not about to tell you I don't associate with people of a certain social class or with questionable reputations. Don't go thinking that's what this is, alright? But everyone knew that girl was wild. Everyone knew she didn't have any boundaries." He stops moving. "I mean, maybe she felt sorry for him because of his head injury, I don't know."

I struggle to catch up. "What do you mean?"

"You're talking about the night I found them together at the old barn, right?"

"You mean after she skipped town," I say, and hope my voice sounds more normal than I feel.

"Yeah." He's movin' again. "I thought I was the only one who knew she was back in town. She swore me to secrecy, so I didn't tell anyone. She was kind of scary."

I stare him down. "Did your brother know you saw him that night?"

He shakes his head back and forth. "No. She's the only one who saw me. He was still inside the barn."

"And you don't know what it was about."

"I figured they were, you know…"

I can't help it. It's so frustratin'. "Right. Because the only reason Marlena would talk to any guy was about sex," I say in a tone that makes me feel like a Sunday School teacher, but I don't care. I'm so tired of everyone's opinion of her.

He goes back to his desk chair. "I don't know, maybe." He searches my face. "Why you bringing all this up now? What's it have to do with anything? Is Marlena back in town?"

"No," I say, but it feels like a lie. Even though she's gone, she's back in full force. And just like every conversation I had with her back in the day, which were few, every one I've had about her leaves me with more questions and no answers.

"Where was your brother the night he fell off the scaffolding?" I ask with my hand on glass doorknob of Gary's office.

"Why does it matter?"

"It's a simple question."

"Haven't you read the police reports? Why are you asking me this?"

"I didn't know the police were involved," I answer. "I was in high school then."

"Deputy Parks is the one who found him. He picked him up, drove him downtown for all of ten minutes, and then he brought him to my parents."

"He didn't call your dad to tell him Hamilton was with him?"

"No. Because Hamilton was eighteen then. The deputy didn't have to bring him home. He did my dad a favor."

"When did he go to the hospital?"

He sighs. "They waited longer than they should have, but Hamilton was arguing with them the whole time, saying he was fine. He didn't want to go to the hospital. He insisted on taking a shower, which was the dumbest thing ever. Like any emergency room is gonna care if a person comes in there covered with dirt."

"He didn't tell you what happened."

His eyes widen. "He couldn't tell anyone what happened because he couldn't remember. He had amnesia or whatever."

"But he told you he didn't want to go to the hospital," I reason.

"Yeah," he says in a much quieter voice that sounds like an admission of guilt. "Whatever my brother did or didn't do, I'd say he's paid the price. He works for my uncle laying brick all day because he can't do anything else. His memory is shot. Sometimes he'll forget what he's doing in the middle of what he's doing."

"Thanks for the peas, Gary, and thanks for bein' honest with me," I say, because I don't know what else to say. It's obvious Gary thinks his brother is guilty, of how much though, that's the question.

11

reread my history notes for the twentieth time. It feels so wrong studying for a history test when Meagan is missing, and no one gives a crap. I shove the thought of kissing Conrad from my brain. Mostly. He's unlike any boy I've ever known. He wasn't all handsy. He didn't keep coming at me. He's the one who broke our kiss which would be more embarrassing except that he was thinking about the investigation. But still. Does that mean I'm a bad kisser, or does it mean I've never kissed an intellectual before, someone who thinks about more than just chemistry? Or maybe I'm just not the girl for him. Why do I care? I kissed him because I felt bad that I made him feel bad. Right?

"Focus, Susan, and stop thinking about things you don't need to think about," I say, right about the time I see someone outside my window. I hold in a shriek when I see Meagan's face. I rush to open it. She climbs in. She has no shoes. Her hair looks wet beneath her hoodie. I try to look her over without being obvious about it. If she were any other girl, I would hug her. But she's not. She's the untouchable Meagan. She's always chill. So why is she crying?

Her hand goes across her face. "It's raining outside," she states. I look past her. I see no raindrops on my window. I say nothing.

"Do you have anything to eat?"

I go for my backpack snacks. She takes them from me. I look

the other way as she rips into them like she's a starving animal. "What are they saying?"

My mind races. "Who?"

"The cops."

"They told me I was the last one to see you alive. They want to know how your phone got in the river."

She coughs a little. I grab my water bottle and hold it out. She sips on the straw. This is so weird. The Meagan I know flipped out about drinking after anyone. "That one's on you," is all she says

I can't believe I'm going to ask this, but I can't not. "Why did you let me throw you over?"

Her green eyes run me through. "Why didn't you go over with me?"

"I was just doing what he told me to do," I plead.

She doesn't blink. There's no change in her flat expression. "So was I."

"Who is he?"

She shakes her head back and forth. "Huh uh. Nope. I'm not answering that."

"Why are you here?"

"I'm hungry." She looks around the room. "Do you have any cash?"

"I have a debit card."

"I can't use that. They'll trace it."

"Who?"

"I can't say."

This is maddening. She's so frustrating. I'm so angry. "I thought you were dead," I say and my voice breaks.

Her eyes stay on whatever she's looking at, which is everything but me. "It felt like you killed me."

Her words hurt. So much. "Is that why you've been playing dead? Was it leading up to whatever this is," I demand. "Do you want me to forfeit, 'cause I forfeit, okay? You win. Game over."

Her eyes meet mine. There's something I've never seen before in them. Fear and desperation. "This isn't a game, Susan. This is *my life*. Did you really think I would go this far for a game?"

I'm so lost. I don't understand why she won't tell me what's going on. I don't know what she wants me to do. "What are you doing here?" I ask again, because I'm tired of asking questions she won't answer.

"I just told you. I need food. I need money." She whips out a tracker phone. "I have two minutes. Then I have to go."

"Is he out there?" I ask as I look out into the darkness, but not too hard. I don't know that I really want to see more I'll have to answer for.

She steps closer and closer until her garlic Chex Mix breath hits me in the face. "You have to figure this out, Susan. I need you. No one else cares."

I hate her words. They give me self-confidence, but they're also suffocating. "He was right. You are an isolator and an instigator. Why should I help you? All you do is push everyone I care about away from me."

She grabs a hold of my hand and squeezes. "I can't talk about that right now, Susan. Please help me. I don't have anyone else."

"You have him," I accuse.

She laughs. "He's not here to help me. He's here for what he can get."

"From you?" I ask, even though I hate it. "Is he doing things to you?"

She shakes her head. "No, no. It's not like that." She coughs. "If it was, I wouldn't be asking you for money."

Her words make me want to vomit. I run to the closet and dig out my coffee can of cash.

"Then what is it?" I ask as I hand it to her. "Here. It's all I've got."

"Thank you," she says. It sounds so strange coming from her.

"You said you needed it."

"I do," she says, and I feel bad for questioning her about it. It's the first time she's asked me for anything.

"It's what he can get because of me," she says in a voice as quiet as a whisper, as if he can somehow hear her. What does that mean?

She slips out my window. I watch from across the room as her black hair fades into the night. It's a good minute before I go to the window and shut it with trembling hands while standing off to the side. If there's someone or something out there, I don't want to know.

I think of Conrad. I glance at my watch. It's almost eleven o'clock. I Snap him. "I heard from M."

"When?"

"Just now."

"What did she say?"

"She asked for my help."

"How do you know it was her?"

I look around the room. I can't believe she was just here. She left no trace, not even a wet footprint on the floor. She wasn't wearing any shoes. I close my eyes and listen. I hear nothing but the sound of losing my sanity. My eyes fly open. There's no rain on my window. I run to the window and stick my hand outside. Dry, cool, night air is all I feel. I stare out into the quiet, dark night. There's no trace of anyone anywhere. Am I hallucinating?

She was just here. I saw her. I talked to her. I felt her eyes on me when I walked into the closet. I need to find a new hiding place for my cash in case she comes back.

My phone buzzes again. It's Conrad. He's Facetiming me. I can't believe how good it feels to see his face. "Hello?" he says.

"She climbed in my window and came in my room," I reply.

"But you're on the second story."

That's why I felt no rain. The way the house is built, it doesn't always hit my window.

"There's a tree outside. She must have climbed it."

"What did she say?"

"She wanted food and money."

"And that's it?"

"She said she didn't want my debit card because it's traceable."

"She doesn't want to be found by the cops."

I'm so stupid. "I guess not. She asked me what the cops said."

"See? She's up to something bad."

"I don't know. She seemed scared. I mean, I told her if this is a game, I quit, and she wins. She said it wasn't. She acted surprised that I would even say that."

"And you believe her?"

"She said I was the only one who can help her."

"See? I told you. She's isolating you. This is gas-lighting or manipulation."

"I'm not saying you're wrong, but what if she really needs help? What if there are other reasons she can't go to the cops?"

"Like what?"

"I don't know, but she also said the man isn't hurting her, but he's keeping her because of what he can get because of her."

"What the heck does that mean?"

"I don't know. You're the detective."

"If he's keeping her but he's not hurting her, and she willingly goes back to him, she could have Stockholm syndrome."

I consider his diagnostic statement. "It's not been long enough for her to have that. She hasn't even been gone for two days. It's like you said. That's why no one is putting up missing posters or whatever."

"Are you going to let this go now?"

"She asked for my help."

"You're a sophomore in high school. What are you supposed to do that the cops can't do?"

He has a point. "I don't know."

"Aren't you supposed to be studying for a history test?"

"I thought you said you weren't stalking me," I tease. I can't believe I'm joking about stalking.

"Padrick has the same class as you. Don't flatter yourself," he replies. Ouch.

"I'm trying, but it's hard. Meagan is in serious trouble. It's hard to concentrate when all I can think about is trying to figure out what is going on with her."

"You should feel better since you saw her, though. Like she can't be in that much danger if she climbed in your window."

"But she went back to him."

"Exactly."

There's too much to think about, and I can't do it when we're talking. "I think I'm gonna go now," I say.

"Alright. Bye."

He ends the call as quickly and randomly as it started. Conrad's one word response about Meagan returning to her captor makes my brain hurt. I question everything all over again. Am I so close that I can't see the whole picture? Why would Meagan want me to think she is dead, only to tell me a day later she's alive? And why would she come back here only to leave again? Conrad is a rational, logical person. He's not wrong. She can't be in that much danger. If she was, the man with the gun wouldn't let her out of his sight. Unless he's threatening her somehow. What if he's telling her he'll hurt me or my parents if she doesn't do what he says? But if any of that's true, who is he, and what does he want?

My thoughts return to the last conversation I had with Dad. There's something he knows about Meagan he's not saying, but how do I find out if he won't tell me?

I text Conrad before I lose my train of thought. It's not weird that I'm texting him close to midnight. This is work. I groan inwardly. I can't believe I'm calling it work, except I can. Meagan is work.

SUSAN:

I think my dad knows something important that he's not saying. How do I find out?

CO:

Does he have an office in your house?

SUSAN:

Yes.

CO:

Does it have a filing cabinet or a desk?

Conrad is so good at this.

SUSAN:

Yes.

CO:

We need to get in there ASAP.

SUSAN:

I think I could go in there when they're asleep.

CO:

No. Don't do that. They might catch you, and if they do, they'll totally know.

SUSAN:

When then?

CO:

Tomorrow. We'll go during during the lunch hour.

SUSAN:

How? I don't have a car.

CO:

Do you have a license?

SUSAN:

Yes.

CO:

Why don't you have a car?

SUSAN:

My parents said I don't need one unless I have a job.

CO:

Harsh.

That's what I thought at first, but it's hard to argue with Dad's logic. There is no reason for me to have a car if I can't put gas in it.

SUSAN:

Practical, Dad said.

CO:

> Well, you can drive Padrick's car. I'll get the keys.
> Meet me outside tomorrow at 0'eleven-hundred.

SUSAN:

11 a.m.?

CO:

> That's what I just said.

SUSAN:

That's not at all what you said. We aren't in the
army.

CO:

> Shut up and soldier on if you want to get this
> thing going.

SUSAN:

What if I find out something I don't want to
know?

CO:

> Susan.

SUSAN:

What?

Bubble, bubble, bubble. My stomach is in knots wondering
what Conrad's going to tell me that is taking so long to type. It's
probably going to be another scathing message about how I put so
much effort into a friendship with Meagan which isn't really a
friendship because she's so awful. And he's not wrong. But she
has no other friends. I'm it. And I don't think she means to be as
tiresome as she is. She can't help herself. She's a survivor. She's
never known what a healthy relationship feels like. She doesn't
know you can hang out just to hang out, that not everything is a
game or something to be gained, and that you don't trick people
you love because that's not normal.

CO:

> There's nothing you can accomplish with worrying about something you can't change. Get back to studying for your test. I'm sure Mrs. H will feel no sympathy if you fail her class because you are worried about Meagan, her least-favorite student.

I read his text twice. It calms me down. I should have known Conrad wouldn't yell at me. I guess I'm too used to Meagan. I sigh as I send him rolling eyes emoji.

SUSAN:

She's everyone's least-favorite student.

CO:

> Gee. Do you see the common denominator here? Surely not everyone is out to get Meagan.

SUSAN:

Shut up, Co. I'm studying.

I can't believe I'm smiling. My best friend is missing. I'm about to break into my dad's study. All I can think of is Conrad and his friendly smile. He's kind of cute. I can't wait for tomorrow.

12

DAY FOUR

he bell rings. I do my best not to sprint out the side doors of the school. My eyes scan the crowded parking lot. I have no idea what Padrick drives. A honking startles me. I keep looking and try to figure out what direction it came from. My eyes go down the line of cars but stop when the lights flash on and off. I feel so sneaky as I hurry across the lot. Conrad smiles from where he sits in the driver's seat. He crawls over the console when I approach the side of the car. I slip inside. "You sure your brother doesn't mind?" I ask as I put it in reverse and start backing up.

"I think he'd be fine with it. I didn't really ask."

I tap the brakes. "What?"

"I lifted his spare key. He doesn't need his car until after school, so it doesn't matter. What he doesn't know won't hurt anything." He taps my knee with his pencil. It feels so personal. "Come on. Keep it moving. We don't have much time."

I swat him and his pencil back to his side of the car. "Fine. Just don't touch me."

The end of his pinkie brushes my shoulder. It's so light I almost don't feel it. "Start moving and I'll stop touching you."

I start backing up. He gives me a squeeze. "Hold up. Someone's walking." He leans toward me again. "Did you not check your mirrors? I thought you said you know how to drive."

His scolding is as annoying as the effect his pinkie has on my shoulder, not to mention his face being way too close to mine. I shove him in the side of his head.

"It doesn't matter if you don't like my driving, Co. You're too young to get out of the parking lot," I snark as I back up once more before putting it in drive. "At least your brother drives a car that doesn't stand out."

"Was that a compliment or an insult?"

I glance over at him while we drive down the road. "It was a compliment." It's too quiet. "What are we looking for?"

"I have no idea. I'm thinking anything that has to do with Meagan."

"And it's just going to be lying around on Dad's desk."

"Do you have a better suggestion on where to start?"

I feel bad for being so rude. I don't know why I'm being so ugly to him. It probably has something to do with the fact that he insulted my driving. I'm not about to tell him I almost backed into someone because he distracted me. "No."

"Okay then." He turns on the radio. "How do you feel about the history test?"

I shrug. "I'm glad it's over. I think I did okay. I kind of like history."

"I kind of like *our history*," he says all flirty-like. I think he's kidding. I'm not sure. This is too weird. I'm not used to Co being so whatever this is.

"You're going to *be history* if you don't stop talking about something that isn't there," I warn.

His back straightens along with the rest of him. I feel bad, but not bad enough. I'm not here for anything but Meagan. I clear my throat. "Thanks for letting me drive your brother's car," I offer.

"What do I care? It's not my car," he grumps.

Way to go, Susan. Way to be a real fun-sucker. Meagan's accusatory voice goes off in my head like an alarm bell.

If she were me and she was involved in this caper, she'd be like in hyperdrive. Anything that was something a person should not do, she was super excited to do. The realization hits me right between the eyes. My foot hits the brakes in the middle of the street. I pull off to the side and stare at my hands on the wheel.

"What am I doing?" I say more to myself than to Conrad who sits in silence beside me. "What if this is another one of her games? She says it isn't, but what if she's crying wolf?" I turn to Conrad with tears in my eyes. I hate crying in front of people. *Fricking Meagan.* "How will I know?" I demand.

He lets out a sigh. "I don't know, Susan, but we don't have time for this. Either we go now, or we go back to school."

He's right. I know he is, but I need more time to decide. I can't believe I'm going to break into my dad's desk. What if there are other things in there I don't want to see that have nothing to do with her? I'm pretty sure there isn't. I'm just saying. I take a deep breath and put the car in drive. "The only thing worse than getting into my dad's stuff is knowing I could have tried to help her, and I didn't," I say aloud.

"Right," Conrad replies. It's only one word, but he may as well be screaming "wrong" in my face like super obnoxious Jim Carrey. Conrad doesn't agree with me about any of this, but at least he's here. My face heats when I think of what that might mean. I'm paying him, and he loves adventure, but still. I can't help but wonder if at least part of him is here just for me.

I pull up to my house. It feels so weird coming here in the middle of the day. We rush the back door. I turn my key in the lock. We walk into Dad's office. I hesitate for half a second before I close the door. Something about leaving it open creeps me out. Conrad sits in Dad's chair. He opens drawers, rifles through them, and goes right to the next one. It's like I'm frozen as I stand here. Watching. His eyes blink in my direction. "Get in the file cabinets."

"Right." I yank the drawer so hard it flies out at me and hits me in the lip. My eyes water. My hand automatically goes to my lip. I'm such a clutz.

"Be quiet," he scolds from somewhere behind me.

"Right," I say again. "Sorry." I flip through Dad's files. I have no idea what I'm looking for. This was the worst idea in the world. "Correspondence. Taxes. Susan's college fund." I will the words to go away, but there they are, right in front of me, written in bold, black Sharpie on colorful tabs, confirming what a horrible daughter I'm being by snooping in Dad's carefully laid financial plans for my future. What am I doing going through his stuff when all his hard work is focused on benefiting me?

"Why is this drawer locked?" Co's question interrupts my internal dilemma.

I turn around and head toward him. "What do you mean?"

He tugs on the bottom drawer. "This one. It's locked."

I stare at the outside of it. "It's not locked. It can't be. There's no place to put a key."

He sits back in the chair. "Fine. You try to open it."

I grab a hold and pull. It doesn't budge. "Maybe it's jammed."

He shakes his head. "I don't think so."

I drop to the floor and lay on my back. "What are you doing on the floor, Susan?"

I glance up at him and tell myself I'm not as lame as I look as I return to inspecting a drawer like I know what I'm doing when in reality I have no clue. "I'm looking for a mechanism that keeps it from opening."

"Oh. That's not a bad idea."

"I know," I say as I shine my phone light as best I can at the underside of the drawer handle. There's a tiny something in there. I see it. I run my fingers along the underside, feeling for a lever or whatever, like when you open the hood of your car. "It can't be too microscopic. Dad's fingers are bigger than mine," I mutter as I keep trying. After a few minutes of memorizing the drawer by feel, I stop trying. Nothing is working. "I don't know," I say as I sit up and move backwards.

Conrad kicks the front of the drawer hard with his foot. It falls open. "Ha," he says as he leans over it at the same time I do. We bonk heads. He sits up. "Sorry. Go ahead. It's your dad's office."

"Thanks," I murmur as I dig through the folders. My eyes light up when I see Certificate of Live Birth. I pull it out and slap it on the desk. "Mary Anne O'Reilly," I say. "Who is that? Why would he have this in his desk?" I turn to Co. "What is going on?"

He coughs. "I'm going to take a wild guess and say Meagan's real name is Mary Anne. Take a picture of it and then we need to put it back exactly how it was. We don't want him knowing we were here." His eyes fly over the paper. I can't see anything. I'm still blinded by the fact that Meagan lied to me about her name. "That's interesting."

"What?"

"There's no father written on the birth certificate."

"I thought they had to," I respond.

"Not necessarily."

I snap a pic of my own before shoving the paper back in the folder. I tidy things up as best I can while trying to remember how they were. I feel like I don't have a fricking clue. I can't believe Meagan lied to me about her name. I can't believe my parents did the same thing. I wonder how much Mom knows. She wouldn't keep all this from me, would she? And if she doesn't know, has Dad known all along? My heard hurts from all this craziness. If Dad knows who Meagan really is, what does that mean?

We walk out to the car in silence. I drive back to school in a daze. "Do you want me to wait until you're with me to investigate further?" Conrad's voice sounds like he's speaking through a tunnel.

"What?"

"Their names. I'm gonna look up their names."

"Oh, yeah." I put the car in park. "Why are you doing that?"

"To see if I get a hit. Like news headlines."

"Oh, yeah."

"Are you okay?"

I bite my lip. "She didn't tell me her name. I thought we were friends." My voice breaks. I want to stop, but I can't. My emotions get the better of me. "I'm so stupid. I gave everyone up for a girl who lied to me about her name." I'm yelling now. Tears roll down my cheeks. Snot threatens to drip from the end of my nose. I'm a disgusting mess. I bury my head in my hands. "I don't under-stand. Why would she do this to me?"

Conrad reaches for me. I back away so fast I bump my head on the window like an idiot. "I hope that hurt," he states in a flat tone.

I laugh and cry at the same time. "Thanks a lot, you jerk."

His hand is on the door handle. "I'm just trying to be nice. This isn't easy for me." He clears his throat. "Girls crying in cars isn't something I know much about."

I pull my hoodie over my head, grab the napkin I spy on the car floor, and wipe my nose with it before shoving it in the side door. I pull my strings as tight they will go. My face slowly disappears. I feel a little better as I close my eyes and try to think. "Meagan, or Mary Anne, or whatever the hell her name really is, could be in serious trouble, and all I can think about is crying over not knowing her name," I muse.

He laughs. I so want to punch him right now. It must show in my face because his hands fly up. "Hey, don't get mad at me. You're just like back and forth like a pendulum. First you're mad at her for lying to you, and now you're berating yourself for being selfish." My eyes bug. "Which you're not. I mean, she's in the middle of a crisis. This is true. But you're entitled to your anger over her lying to you."

His words do nothing but prove that I'm as crazy as I feel. I stare at the darkness of my sweatshirt covering my eyes. "I'm sorry. I just have all these emotions, and they're coming all at once, and I don't know what to think about everything."

He doesn't answer. I think I hear him tapping his fingers on the door. "I hate to say this, but um, we need to go in soon. The bell is going to ring. And you can't wear your hood inside. You'll be sent to the principal's office."

In spite of everything I'm feeling, I giggle at his words. "At least I'd get to go home, but someone would have to come and get me. I don't want to interrupt my parent's workday. This isn't an emergency." Well, it kind of is, but I'm not ready to tell Dad how I know Meagan's name isn't Mary, or that I know he knew the whole time.

I turn to face Conrad. I let go of my strings and loosen my hoodie before tugging it off my head. He reaches over and musses my hair. "You're all staticky."

"It has to be what you said, right? I mean, Mary is Meagan. What other explanation could there be?"

He stares me down. "Other than your dad could be like her baby daddy? I don't know."

I give him a hard shove. "Eww. That's gross. Why would you say that? My dad wouldn't do that."

He shrugs. "I've watched enough Lifetime movies to know that's like a deep, dark secret they hide in desk drawers or what-ever." He wrinkles his nose. "But you're right. Your dad doesn't strike me as the gigolo type. He's not cringey enough to be a serial cheater or whatever."

I open the car door. I can't believe I forgot how weird the things Conrad says are. "Well, that's a relief."

"You're welcome," he offers in a sincere tone, like he doesn't know that suggesting my dad had two children with two women around the same time while being married to one of them, my mother, isn't like super offensive. But then again, I'm the one who told him my dad is lying to me about something.

We walk to school together. It occurs to me that I wouldn't know any of this except for Conrad. "Thanks for going with me," I say, and I mean so much more than that.

He turns to me and smiles. "It was no problem. Snooping is what I'm good at. Someday I want to do it professionally."

I nod my head. "Well, thanks anyway. I don't think I could have done it alone."

He stops in the middle of the sidewalk. We're just a few steps from the building. "Susan, we both know that's not true. If you want to do something, you will. I know you. Nothing scares you."

I don't know what to say to that. I don't know if I believe him, but I'm not about to argue. The bell rings, saving me from further awkwardness. I rush past him. "Better get to class," I call out. "You don't want to be late."

My focus is pretty much shot for the rest of the day. All I can think about is Meagan and why would she lie to me about her first name. I mean, she could have told me her name was Mary Marks, and I never would have suspected a thing. It stings that all this time I've been calling her Meagan. Everything between us feels so fake. Every memory I have of her is ruined. Her name was on every birthday cake she's had since she came to live with us. Every card. Every note I ever wrote to her. This is all so messed up.

I can't believe I'm crying again. This is so dumb. I'm so tired of all the drama. It's exhausting. She's ruining my life. I hurry to the nearest bathroom to wash my face with cold water. I can't walk into class looking like this. I stand in front of the mirror, willing my eyes to be less glassy and bloodshot. Why can't I stop crying? I run more cold water to splash my face again.

Suddenly, I feel like I'm not alone. Someone stands beside me in sparkly red Converse covered with sequins that fit her nonexistent ankles encased in black skinny jeans. Why can't I stop staring at her feet? It has to be Jaz. "Don't pretend to miss her, Susan," she snarks.

Great. This is freaking awesome. I thought my day couldn't get any worse. Memories of her last SnapChat run through my head. She was so cold. Jaz is the last person I want to see. "Of course, I miss her," I manage to say without blubbering as I force myself to look her in the eye. My lower lip won't stop quivering. It's so embarrassing.

"You should be glad she's gone. She was no good for you. All that toxic freak does is drag everyone down."

Her words hurt because they're true. "I can't believe you would say that about her, especially now that she's…" I stop talking. What am I thinking, telling Meagan's business to Jaz, the biggest gossip of them all.

"Now that she's been moved to another foster home? What's the big deal? It's not like you can't look her up." She leans into the mirror, getting so close her breath fogs up the glass before she applies her lip gloss. Her brown eyes meet mine in the mirror. "She won't be callin' you. I'm sure she's already found someone else's life to destroy. You should just forget about her, 'cause she's definitely forgot about you."

All I can think of is Meagan crying in my room. "You don't know everything," I manage, but it sounds weak.

Jaz baps her lips together a few times, looks in the mirror one more time, and turns to face me. Her shiny lips, wingtip eyes, perfect hair, and mean girl face make her look like a meme. "Don't beg for her attention, Susan. It's just embarrassing."

I open my mouth to argue but close it again. There are more

important things to do than stand here and argue with Jaz, a girl who was barely my friend before she let Meagan get between us. The bathroom door closes. Jaz is gone.

I scan the floor for any feet before pushing every stall door open. I'm completely alone. I whip out my phone and start a voicemail to Conrad.

"Who is telling people Meagan moved to another foster home, and why? Why else would Jaz, who knows everybody's business, say that? Someone must have told her something. Unless Jaz started the rumor just to be mean. This is all so tiresome.

If everyone thinks Meagan transferred to another foster home that would explain why no one is looking for her.

Maybe Meagan spread the rumor herself. She could have called in on a pay phone or something crazy like that.

She is really good at imitating other people, especially older ones. Calling herself in to the school for a transfer sounds exactly like something Megan would do.

It's like you said. Meagan obviously doesn't want the cops looking for her. What does she think I can do that no one else can?" I stop talking before the file is so big it can't be sent. I can't believe how fast words flowed from my lips. "C'mon Co. Open it," I mutter. I feel split right down the middle. Part of me wants to

Co replies, "Message received. Meet me in the library in ten."

I jump at his response and try not to think about how much I'm relying on Conrad. He said I could do this alone, but he's wrong. I'm not nearly as strong as he thinks. The library is on the top floor of the high school. I need to get up there. If I use the old stairwells there's no hall monitors.

I find him sitting at a back corner table nose deep in his math book. I sit down across from him. He shoves a notebook my way. "Here. We're studying."

"Am I your tutor?" I ask in a flirty manner.

He stares me down. "Girl, puh-lease. We both know who would be tutoring who. I'm practically National Merit Scholar material."

My face heats at his words. He's not wrong, but still. "Way to be a buzzkill. You don't need to wave your intellectual superiority in my face like that."

He blinks but does not break his stare or facial expression. "I am an investigator. I speak the truth."

I wave my hands as if to clear the air between us. "Yes, the investigation. I've been thinking about this. I want to ask my dad about what we found, but I can't. I'm not ready."

His eyes widen in surprise. "You're seriously going to tell your dad we got into his drawer?"

I draw shapes on the paper. "Not we, Co. Me. I got into his desk drawer."

"You're going to start off a truth-telling conversation with a lie?"

I feel so judged, but he's not wrong. "He lied first."

His fingers tap on the table. "Agreed. Omission is the same as lying."

"But he was trying to protect me."

"Except that she's kind of missing, and people are covering it up. Everything is different now. If he knows she's not really missing, what does that mean? Does he know about the man with the gun? And if he doesn't know anything about it, then he thinks she's missing but he doesn't care. So how is that better?"

His blunt comments make my head spin. All of them make too much sense and none of it is reassuring. "I don't know," I answer as I bury my face in my hands. "But in a horrible way, this makes so much sense."

"What do you mean?" His soft voice prompts me to keep talking, even though it's only going to get more awkward.

"It's just, all of this drama is what life with Meagan is like," I say as I force myself to look him in the eye. "I have more than one reservation about talking to Dad about what we found in the desk. Asking him about what's in his desk drawer is just going to get him and Mom into another fight, and things have been mostly relaxed at home since Meagan left. It's weird. It's like I forgot what calm feels like. There's no drama. There's no conflict. There are no arguments between Mom and Dad about Meagan and it's so nice." I pause. "I can't believe I'm saying all this. She's missing."

He touches my hand holding the pen. "It's okay to let it out. Who am I gonna tell?"

It's insane that I'm smiling after what I just said. Or that this boy gives me serious butterflies when whatever this is between us should be the last thing on my mind. "I'm so glad you're not Jaz," I half joke.

Confusion fills his face. "I'm not even gonna ask what that means."

I sit back in my chair. He looks wounded when my hand moves away from his. "You said you won't tell anyone, and Jaz popped into my head, because she tells everyone everything all the time," I explain.

"Are you worried that you can't see straight because Meagan is so much?" he asks, letting me off the hook. He's so sweet.

I can't believe I'm thinking what I'm thinking about him. I shouldn't be thinking anything about him. "So much," I murmur.

"Excuse me?"

Focus, Susan. Seriously. "Meagan," I blurt while my mind tries to stop thinking about how nice his smile is, and how concerned he looks, but also how there's something that tells me he knows exactly why I'm having trouble focusing. "Like sometimes Mom and Dad would go for days without speaking because they were fighting about a decision that was tied to Meagan. And *she* would walk around like she owned our house."

He nods. "Because she kind of did, and she enjoyed it." His statement is more of a fact. There's no resentment in his tone. I wish I could I feel the same.

"The majority of my parents' emotions were a direct response to whatever was going on in Meagan's life," I explain. "Dad quit the bowling team because of Meagan. He quit his membership in the community men's group because of Meagan. He started working shorter hours because Mom couldn't handle Meagan's attitude or her behaviors when she didn't get what she wanted. Meagan was constantly sneaking out of the house. It's like she had no fear." I should stop talking, but it's like I have verbal diarrhea.

"She had a knack for disruption," I continued. "If I had anything scheduled, like ballet class or piano lessons, it was inevitable that Meagan would disappear about the time we had to leave so I would not be late. Mom would get so furious. After the third or fourth lesson I missed, I was begging Mom to let me quit. Now that I'm not a little girl anymore, I see that Mom probably felt like she was losing the invisible war Meagan started. Meagan was a champion at passive resistance. She would not tell my mom "no," she would just do things to make it impossible for us to get to practice on time because we were looking for her. Mom cried when she told me I was done with ballet. She did it again about the piano lessons." My voice catches. I wipe away a tear. This is so stupid.

"I'm sorry," he says, and I don't feel so dumb. "I'm sorry she ruined those memories you should have had with your mom."

"It's just. Meagan never acted like she felt bad about any of it."

"Maybe she was hurting, and she didn't know how to act any other way."

"I guess. Meagan is just so young to be so heartless. I still remember it like it was yesterday. She just sat there in the backseat of the car when Mom made a tearful apology both times to me about making me quit. Meagan didn't say a word. She just stared through my mother as if she wasn't there while I told my mom that it wasn't that big of a deal, that I was fine, that it didn't matter that much to me."

"And was that the truth?"

"Eventually," I answer while feeling like a selfish baby, the very thing Meagan called me when she caught me crying in my room while shoving my piano books to the bottom of a box in the back of my closet. I knew Meagan was wrong, but she had a way of making her problems front and center. Her parents were gone. She was an orphan. Her struggle was real. Mine wasn't. She was so convincing.

"It wasn't right for her to take your dreams and your enjoyment," Conrad says. I almost love him. Whoa.

"I guess not," I answer. "But it doesn't matter now. That's all in the past."

"It doesn't have to be."

What? "What do you mean?"

"You could still take ballet. You could still learn to play the piano."

"I'd be way behind."

He shrugs. "That doesn't matter. Don't you watch The Late Show? That Ken doll guy is a freaking actor. He makes a ton of money. He takes ballet classes with little girls."

I wrinkle my nose. "And that's not creepy?"

He laughs. "First of all, he's a dad. He's *LaLa Land* Ryan. It's not creepy. Secondly, stop changing the subject or dismissing the point I'm trying to make. You know what I'm saying. You can do lots of things. You're fifteen. Your outlook can't be this dark."

Insecurity fills me. "I'd be so far behind," I repeat.

"It's not a race, Susan. Mr. M gives piano lessons. Go and see him sometime."

"I don't have time for that."

"He does it during study hall." He taps a finger on the table. "People make time for things that matter to them."

"Fine. I'll think about it. Okay? But right now, we need to focus on Meagan."

He shifts in his chair. "I know something," he says all quiet-like. It's so sexy.

"What do you know?" I can't believe my level of excitement.

"It's about her mom."

I hate the way I love the way he's dragging this out, torturing me. "What is it?"

His stare doesn't waver. "It changes everything."

A delicious sense of panic fills me. I don't want to know, but I must know. "What?" I find myself whispering as I lean forward.

"Once you know, you can't not know, and it's big."

My throat is dry. "How big?" What can be bigger than discovering she has a whole other identity?

"Like meteorite-destroying-a-planet big."

My stomach bottoms out. I'm like freezing cold. "You totally suck," I say.

His look of innocence hits me right in the gut. "What? Why?" He sounds all surprised, but his growing grin betrays him. He knows exactly what he's doing.

"I can't walk away from you now."

"That's the plan," he mutters. I think, *Whoa*. Nerd boy has a whole level of deception I did not anticipate.

"What is it?" I demand.

He opens his binder, takes out a manila envelope and slides it across the table to me. I feel so undercover. We both stare at the envelope lying face down. "Open it," he says.

I turn it over and mess with the tack before ripping the paper across the top. I reach inside and pull out a photo of a woman sitting on a park bench. I don't think I've seen her before, but there's something so familiar. "I don't understand."

"That's her mom."

I look closer. There's a definite resemblance in her mother's face shape and hairline. "Okay. Well, what does an old photo have to do with what's going on now?"

"That photo was taken a month ago."

It falls from my shaking fingers. "Meagan's not an orphan?"

He takes a deep breath. "I guess not."

I tear my eyes from the photo to look at him. "Do you think Meagan knows?"

"I don't know."

It's quiet for too long. I want to say something. Anything. But I don't know what to say. My mind races. I can't believe her mom is alive, and if she is alive, why did she let Meagan think she's dead? "Do you think your dad knows?"

Oh, crap. I didn't think about that. A different kind of dread washes over me. "I don't know."

I take out my phone to take a picture of the picture. Conrad snatches it back. "Don't," he says.

The urgency in his tone stops my irritation. "Why not?"

He shoves the photo back it the envelope. "I don't know yet. I just have this feeling."

"Are you serious?"

The bell rings. He shoves his binder back in his backpack. "Why would I joke about your safety?"

I stand up out of my chair. "You told me I could do anything I put my mind to."

He nods his head again. "That's what I'm afraid of."

We walk across the library, barely noticing the other students as we take the nearest exit. "I can take care of myself, you know," I say as we jog down the steps.

He takes my hand. He stops mid-step. I do the same. He leans against the wall and tugs me to him. We stand toe-to-toe. "I know you're okay on your own, but maybe I'm not."

His words catch me off guard. They catch up to me about the time his lips find mine. Who knew blunt honesty was so irresistible? His kiss is straight up fire. Who knew plain-clothes Conrad who spends all his time reading books and news headlines had serious game? The bell rings again. We both jump. "We're gonna be late to class."

He glances at his watch. "I've never been tardy."

I can't stop staring at his lips. What is going on with me? "Rebel," I say before leaning in to give him one more quick peck. "Get to class."

"I'm going," he says as he continues down the steps. I start after him.

"Where are you going, Susan? You have Spanish Two. It's upstairs."

I stop moving. "Stalker," I answer, but in a teasing manner.

"I'm your number one fan and you love it," he yells right before I hear the door close.

I walk down the hall in a daze. I've got it bad for Conrad, and he knows it. And I don't care.

My new feelings for Conrad and the photo plague me the rest of the day. I snap pictures of the whiteboard every hour so I don't forget anything. My inability to concentrate is off the charts. The end of the day is finally here.

"Where you going, Susan? We have a yearbook meeting," Evie reminds me as she pops up by my side out of nowhere.

"Oh, yeah."

I have no ride home now. This sucks. I should text my parents, but I'm angry at Dad for everything he's kept from me. I may have been eleven when she came to stay with us, but I'm fifteen now.

SUSAN:

Got a meeting after school.

MOM:

But you have therapy.

I glance at the calendar. I've got an hour in between study hall, my last hour, and yearbook.

SUSAN:

Can you see if Kerin can see me an hour earlier?
Please. It's my study hall. I don't have anything
to do anyway.

MOM:

Fine.

SUSAN:

Thanks. Let me know.

MOM:

K.

13

Badge 343

t's not like me to use my job to barge into the middle of people's workdays, but I've got a fifteen-year-old girl gone missin', and no one seems to care except me. It's my job.

I've called Mr. Tripp's office twice. He's either dodgin' me or... if I know him like I think I do, he's dodgin' me. I shoot his receptionist a friendly smile. "I'm here to see your boss."

Her eyes go back and forth just enough to tell me she's really nervous. "I'm afraid he's on a phone call. Please have a seat, sir."

It's not an unreasonable request, but the thought that this woman and her boss think they can put the law on hold pushes all the wrong buttons. I move past her desk and down the hallway. I pause outside the closed door long enough to find out he actually is on a phone call. I turn the knob. The door swings open. "Carley, I'm on a call," he says before turnin' to take me in. He hangs up the phone.

"Hi," I say before closin' the door in Carley's face and not feelin' the least bit bad about it. I cross the room and sit down in a chair. "I'll try not take up more of your time than necessary," I continue. "I'm sure you're a very busy man."

He nods his head like a bobble head. "Sheriff, what a nice surprise."

I tilt my head to the side. "Is it?"

"Why do you say that?" Either he's hot blooded, or the man is extremely nervous. Sweat beads above his lip.

"I find it odd that your foster daughter is missin', and you and your wife are just going about like everythin' is business as usual."

He frowns. "It's no secret that girl runs away. She does whatever she wants whenever she wants. I'm about done letting my daughter follow her into no end of trouble."

"I'm sorry your daughter got into trouble. I'm sure that's hard for any father to see," I empathize. "But that doesn't change the fact that a girl is missin'. I think your daughter may have been the last person to see her alive."

"Just what are you saying, Sheriff?"

"I'm saying what I just said, Jeff."

"I'd think twice before pointing fingers. I know a lot of people in this town. They have some pull. I hear you're up for re-election soon."

I lean back in my chair. "Are you threatenin' me?"

His face turns even darker. "Certainly not. I just don't like the idea that you are trying to incriminate my daughter when she didn't do anything wrong."

"You're an outsider, is that right?" I ask.

He grips the edge of the desk. "Are you implying my daughter is guilty because she's not from here? Is that what this is? Of all the people in this town, you're the last person I thought would pull that kind of stunt."

"Jeff," I say in the same tone of voice I used to de-escalate a man who was beatin' on his wife when I kicked in his door. "I'm askin' if you knew Marlena O'Reilly."

He blinks a few times, as if he's trying to focus. "Yeah, she's Meagan's mother," he fires back.

"But did you know her personally?"

"No."

"So you didn't know Marlena's mother lives about five miles out, on the edge of town?"

His eyes bug. "Hell, no." He stares back at me. "Does the grandmother know her granddaughter lives here?"

I nod my head. "She met her once, the day she came to live with you."

"Did Meagan know who she was meeting?"

I shake my head again. "No." He gives me a look of disgust. "That's the way it had to be," I explain. "Does your wife know you how much money you made when you took Meagan in?"

He shrugs his shoulders. "What's between my wife and me isn't really your concern," he says givin' me a look of warning. "That's the way it had to be," he continues, throwin' my words in my face.

"So she doesn't know." I store that information away for future reference should I need it. I'm surprised at how disappointed I am to find out his marriage is so flawed, but that has nothin' to do with what is going on right now.

"What is this visit about?" he demands.

"I need to find the girl as soon as possible, and I think you're withholdin' information. At the very least you're not actively lookin' for a girl who was in your care before she went missin'. I wouldn't be doin' my job if I didn't find that a bit alarmin'."

"She's a runaway, Sheriff. I wish I could tell you more, but I can't. Like I said before, I have the safety of my own family to think about. Searching for a girl who jeopardized the wellbeing of my daughter is not going to be high on my priority list. I'm a father first. I won't apologize for that."

"But you'll keep the money that helped pay off your house and who knows what else," I fire back at him. "It's nice to know where your *priorities* lie."

"You're not a father or a husband. You don't know what it's like."

His words hit me hard. Judgin' by his look of triumph, I think that was his intention. "I don't have to be either to be a decent human bein', Jeff. You should try it," I say as I stand up. "Don't even think about goin' anywhere. I'll keep in touch. If I find you've done anythin' outside the law, I'm nailin' your greedy ass to the wall."

"You would've taken the money too," he protests right before I open his door to let myself out.

"I didn't think you were the type of man who would turn in his morals for a bundle of cash, Jeff. I guess I was wrong about you."

"I haven't done anything wrong," he yells at my retreating back.

"You haven't done anythin' right either," I reply in kind as I pass by Carley's desk, ignorin' curious looks from people sittin' in the waitin' room. I suppose I should feel bad for announcin' Jeff's major personality flaws in his place of business in front of potential clients, but I can't.

Meagan might have sold out the Tripps, but at least she did it for love of family. All she gambled was her pride. Jeff sold out for money, and he let a teenage girl throw herself to the wolves to do it.

14

SNACK TIME - (NOT) FUNYONS

ou're particularly chipper today," Kerin, my therapist, says, and she's not wrong. I'm kind of floating on my feelings for Co, and mostly ignoring the part of my life I can't discuss with her, no matter how patient and good of a listener she might be.

"I'm in serious like," I spill, as I flop down on her loveseat.

"Did you and Ryan get back together? I knew he'd come to his senses."

I can't believe how much hearing that doesn't hurt. I have like no feelings about it whatsoever.

"Not exactly," I answer.

"Oh?"

"His name is Co. He's a year younger than me," I say, all embarrassed. "He's a freshman."

She studies me. I feel like bacteria in a microscope. "And this bothers you?"

I shrug my shoulders. "I don't think so. No." I fiddle with a loose string. "Like he's more mature than most of the guys in my high school anyway, so it doesn't seem like he's a freshman."

"Well, maturity is a great quality in a guy."

I nod. "Yeah. I think so."

"So how did you meet?"

I giggle. "Well, he's kind of my first kiss."

Her eyebrows raise. "Really," she says, but it's not a question.

"Yeah. I was like almost thirteen and he was eleven. We rode the bus together. And his brother is my age, and we like the same things, like the same clubs or whatever, so Co was always kind of around."

"You kissed him because he was around?" she questions, but not in an accusing way.

"No. Like, there was this mystery, okay. Like a smalltown hundred-year-old mystery, and he solved it. He's a Nancy Drew type, but he's a guy," I say, because there's nothing girlish about Conrad.

"So he's a Hardy Boy," she says.

"What?"

"*The Hardy Boys* were the guy's detective series, like the equivalent of *Nancy Drew*," she explains.

"Emma Watson's movie had nothing about the Hardy Boys in there," I say.

Kerin laughs out loud. "I forget how old I am and how young you are. *Nancy Drew* and *The Hardy Boys* were books written way back in my day. They came along way before the movie."

"Oh. Well, anyway, that's what he's into. And so..." I stop talking. I'm not about to tell her I hired him because I thought I was an *accessory to murder*. "I don't know. We just started talking, and it kind of turned into something."

"And it's going good," Kerin asks.

I think of our little make out sesh in the library. "Yeah, it's going good."

"Susan," Kerin says in a more serious tone. All the lightness we just had disappears.

"What."

"Your mom says you've had a few big changes in your life recently. Are you ready to talk about any of that?"

I lay back and close my eyes. All I want to do is block out that night, the night I threw my best friend off a bridge and became an *accessory to murder*, except that I'm not. I'm not. I'm not.

His threat carries no weight. She's alive. I grip my jeans with my hands. I wonder what all Mom said to Kerin. I wonder what she knows that she wants me to tell her even though she already knows.

"They say growth comes from change," I say, because I don't know what else to say, and I don't want to talk about this. Not with Kerin. Not in her office. Not while I'm lying on her comfy, plaid loveseat which I'm sure has had many secrets spilled on it, but mine won't be one of them. If I tell Kerin what I know, it could put her in danger.

"Do you feel like you're growing?" she asks.

Yeah. I'm growing more irritated by the second, but I'm sure that's not what she meant. "We'll see," I say all cryptic and cool-like, even though it's the last thing I feel. I feel like I'm going to catch fire and burn to ashes right in front of her. I'm so angry I think I could incinerate this entire room. I know this is therapy, but I can't believe she dropped a truth bomb on me like that. I'm the one who is supposed to lead the discussion. This is my therapy session. Not hers, and certainly not my mother's, even though I'm sure she's paying for it.

I close my eyes again. This sucks. I've just entered a game of silence with my therapist because of my mother inadvertently taking over yet another part of my life. I just want to be myself. I wanted something for myself, something she could not control. And I thought I would find it here. But I can't. I'm forever tied to her. And I know she means well, but sometimes, it's too much.

A tear rolls down my cheek. What is wrong with me? Why am I so angry with my mom when the person I should be angry with, the person who isn't here, the person I can't stop thinking about even though I'm one hundred percent positive I'm the last person on her twisted mind, Meagan Davis, has a chokehold on us all, because we can't let her go. Her absence is just as strangulating as if she were standing here in the room staring down at me telling me what an idiot I am for crying on a stranger's couch.

I'm so lost. I don't know who the enemy is, or maybe I do, and I just don't want to know, because if I'm best friends with the one person trying to destroy me, and I leave everyone else behind for her, what does that make me?

"Time's up," Kerin announces in an annoyed tone, but I can't bring myself to care. She shouldn't have brought Mom into the room or tried to run the session.

"Yep," I agree as I walk out. I've got to stop letting Meagan have such a hold on me, but I don't know how to take my own steps if they lead away from her. How can I save her if I leave her behind?

———

I spy Mom's car in the lot. I'm so mad I could walk the four miles to the school, but then I'd miss yearbook. I open the door and climb in.

"How was it?" Mom wants information I don't want to give.

"It was *my* therapy session," I bark.

She puts the car in drive. "It's nice to know my hard earned money is going to your therapy. You know you're not the only one who could use a nonjudgmental listening ear," she says as she turns out in front of a monster truck. His brakes squeal. The driver lays on the horn.

"Shit," Mom says.

I almost laugh, but I don't dare. His grill fills up our back window. "Did you not see him?" I ask.

She glances over at me as she floors it. "Obviously not."

Minutes later we're at the school. "Are you okay to drive home?" I say, even though I don't know that I want her to answer.

She blinks. "Of course. Why would you ask that?"

Because you almost got us killed by pulling out in front of a truck that took up one-and-a-half lanes of traffic. "No reason. Just, be careful, Mom," I say. I feel terrible for being so angry at her in Kerin's office. I'm a horrible daughter.

"Do you need a ride after yearbook?"

"I think I can find one," I say before closing the door.

She rolls my window down. "Bye, honey. Love you," she calls.

I look back. "Love you too, Mom," I say, and I mean it. And then I feel bad because I think of every day Meagan went without her mom, and how I hated every second I had to share mine with her.

I walk into yearbook. I hate these stupid meetings. Basically, they consist of our clueless president, Gigi, trying to run the meeting when she is like the most unimaginative person in the room. She has the creativity of a brick. This wouldn't bother me so much if she wasn't such a B and didn't claim everyone's ideas as her own, which is the very reason she's president. So maybe she's not as clueless as she appears. I sit down in the last chair near the end of the long table. Conrad slides into the chair next to me. What is he doing here? He's not on yearbook, a fact I think just dawned on Gigi who stares him down with narrowed eyes outlined by her perfect dark lashes. I don't know why she wears makeup. Her face is flawless.

"What are you doing here?"

Please don't let him say something about me, I think, and then I feel terrible for thinking it. "It's not an exclusive club," he argues.

"But the school year has already started."

"And you've had two meetings. The first semester is not over yet. Per school policy number seventeen in the student handbook, I am still allowed to join this group."

"The semester ends tomorrow," red-headed, brown-eyed Evie argues from across the table.

"I was just going to say that, Evie," green eyed Gigi barks.

Evie's eyes water.

"You don't need to yell at her," I scold Gigi.

"I can defend myself," Evie barks at me while wiping a tear from her eye. "You don't need to yell at me," she says to Gigi in a voice so quiet she may as well be in a basement, speaking up through the vents.

"I didn't say you could stay," Gigi's staring at Conrad again with a stare that wilts most students.

He leans back in his chair and crosses his arms on his chest. "Well, I'm not leaving." His foot finds mine beneath the table. *What is going on?*

"Fine. Whatever. I don't have time for this. We have more important matters to discuss." She looks around the table. "Where's Meagan?" she demands.

I open my mouth to answer before closing it again. I glance

around the table. Everyone stares at me. This is so annoying. I so don't believe Gigi doesn't know why Meagan isn't here. She's just being awful because she can be. "She's not here."

"Is she coming to today's meeting?" Gigi fires back.

"Where have you been?" Colin accuses, which is so weird. He has mega feelings for Gigi. He never calls her out.

"What's that supposed to mean?"

"She's gone, Gigi. She doesn't go to school here," Colin replies. My throat tightens. My eyes water. I want to be anywhere but here. Clueless Colin looks over at me. "I'm sorry," he mouths, taking me by complete surprise. He's not usually one to acknowledge other people's feelings.

"Well, that sucks. She was our best digital marketing person."

"I know how to do that," Conrad offers.

Gigi rolls her eyes. "I'm sure you won't come close to what Meagan could do, but I'll take what I can get."

Conrad stands up. "Or I could walk."

Whoa. No one has ever told Gigi no before. *He's so hot.* "Stay," I say. "Please."

He looks down at me. This is so strange. "If you really want me to," he answers, and it feels like he's talking about something other than yearbook.

"Stay and prove her wrong," I challenge. This just got weird. It's just yearbook.

"Yeah. Make Gigi eat her words," Colin taunts, which is just bizarre. His giant crush on Gigi is on its fourth year. He's so desperate it's pathetic. Until today, apparently. Usually, he's bends over backward for her. He agrees with anything she says.

Conrad sits down in the chair once more. I resist the urge to giggle. I can't believe we're talking smack about yearbook. This is hilarious, but it's also fun. I feel all warm and fuzzy when it hits me that Conrad is the reason.

A smile sneaks out of Gigi. "You better live up to your reputation, Conrad," she warns.

"It's Co," Conrad and I say at the same time. I shut my mouth and mostly ignore his eyes on me along with his adorable grin. "I go by Co now," he explains.

"Co," Colin answers. "As in CoCo Chanel?"

"Dude. Did you just reference an old lady perfume to dis me?" Conrad replies.

"Hey," Gigi orders from the end of the table. "First of all, Chanel is all time. Secondly, stop being such *dudes*. I officially call this meeting to order."

"I second it," I answer while trying to ignore Conrad playing footsie with me. Colin leans back in his chair while gripping the edge of the table to keep him from going all the way to the floor. I track his gaze on our feet beneath the table. I scoot sideways in my chair, but it's too late. I see it in his smirk right before the two chair legs hit the floor with a bam and a screech.

Gigi stops midsentence. I have no idea what she was saying. "Colin. Could you not?"

He tears his eyes from mine in super slo mo. "Sorry, Gigi. I guess I was distracted."

He's such a pervy jerk. Colin's hands are making weird motions but I'm pretty sure he's referring to me and Conrad, and I'm pretty sure it's disgusting. My face heats. I glance over at Conrad who stares at Colin like he's an idiot before flipping him two birds. I wish I was that confident.

Gigi clears her throat. "Colin," she says in the voice that tells me she's about to nail him to the wall.

"Yeah," he says as he goes still before sitting up straighter and tries to look all serious. Co lays his birds down.

"Do we need to have an emergency meeting to discuss if either of you are worth putting up with?"

"No."

"Good. We established we raised four thousand dollars last year with our fundraiser and it paid off. We produced a killer yearbook that won state. However, we also lost most of our yearbook staff. We're kind of starting over from scratch. This means we will all be multi-tasking. I will need serious time commitments from all of you. So please think twice about what you sign up for. Once you do, there's no backing out."

Her words are such a relief to hear. Busyness is just what I need, which must be why I'm signing up for like five or six things.

"Slow your roll, girl," Colin comments from across the table. "Leave some for the rest of us to do."

I lay the pen down and scan the paper once more before taking a picture of it with my phone, so I don't forget what I signed up for. "I will, but we all know how *some people* sign up for things and then they don't do them."

"Just like everyone knows I'm the one stuck with getting it done if that happens," Gigi interjects. I close my eyes so they don't bug.

That is so not what happened last year. Three seniors checked out. I did all the work to avoid the wrath of our teacher who threatened to quit and walk out like at least fifteen times. Then Gigi had the nerve to claim my work as hers. It was super annoying.

"Well. You don't have to worry about me," Conrad announces. "If I commit to something, I see it through."

That's like something you say three months into a relationship which I'm not even sure we are in. I can't believe how bad I want him to mean the words he said, but in a different way. I will not be a weirdo love bomber or be taken in by one. But it's not like he's professing his love for me three days after we shared our first kiss, and it's not like we don't know each other. I've kind of known him since he was like eleven. Padrick and I have similar interests. We've been in the same clubs for a while. And Conrad is kind of like his brother's shadow, so he was always sort of there, or was he? Was it more than that and I just didn't notice?

He picks up my pen and scribbles something on my paper. "Need a ride home?"

"Yes," I write back as I try to focus on what Gigi is saying and ignore Colin staring at the notebook lying between Conrad and I. Colin's meaty hands that are as thick and immovable as the rest of him sneak toward it. He's a powerlifter. I jerk the notebook away from his grasp. It falls in my lap. Brickhouse Colin smirks. At this moment, I can't stand him. I wish he would sit somewhere else other than across from me.

"Any ideas?" Gigi's question cuts into my glaring contest with Colin.

"For what?" I ask.

"Did you not hear what I just said?"

"Colin?" I challenge.

"What."

"Do you know what she's talking about?"

It's a low blow to try to deflect Gigi's yelling at me by pointing the finger at Colin, but I'm not the only one not paying attention.

"Gigi wants to know if anyone has ideas for the school carnival this year," Conrad responds. I think I hear a bit of irritation in his tone.

Apparently, Conrad can distract me but no one else can, even though the whole reason Colin is staring at me is because Conrad wrote me a note and I wrote one back. "For what?"

"The theme," she practically yells.

"Why is this decision on us?" I demand.

"It's not," Colin answers. "Gigi is the Junior class president. She's supposed to come up with something, but she can't, so she's asking us."

"Yearbook is all about teamwork. You know that," she argues.

"But the school carnival theme has nothing to do with the yearbook," Conrad argues.

"It will be in the yearbook because there will be lots of pictures from it in there," Gigi insists.

I wave my hands in the air. "Can we just acknowledge that you are asking us to come up with a killer idea that you will claim as your own?" I can't believe I said that out loud.

Gigi looks like someone hit her. "You know what? Fine. I'll figure it out myself."

"We didn't say we wouldn't help you. We're just asking that you admit to us that what Susan said is true," Conrad says.

"And then you'll help me?" Gigi muses.

"Yes," I answer. Why is it so important for me to get her to admit she steals people's ideas? Am I being petty?

Everyone sits nervously in their chairs, anxiously waiting for her admission while staring a hole through the table. Gigi lets out a long, dramatic sigh. "Fine. Maybe sometimes someone else comes up with an idea that I had that I didn't voice before they did, and so I said it was mine."

"Liar," Conrad coughs into his hand.

Gigi smacks the table with her hand. We all jump. She closes her eyes. Her long, skinny fingers wrap around her spaghetti arms. "Sometimes I claim ideas that aren't mine," she says from behind gritted teeth. Her cheeks are pink. Her green eyes burn holes through my forehead. Her ponytail looks extra tight. "Are you happy now?"

"Very," Conrad comments beside me.

I say nothing.

"Now. Who has an idea?" she asks with a smile on her face, but it's forced.

Conrad raises his hand, but I don't know why. He's been speaking freely until now. "Yes, Co?"

"I say Gigi comes up with an idea since she's the president."

She white knuckles the table. Conrad is about to get kicked out of his first yearbook meeting, and he won't be asked back.

I clear my throat. "I think Gigi should be presented with ideas and she can choose the best one."

Colin nods his head like a bobblehead. "Yeah, I agree with Susan. That's an excellent idea," he says and gives me a wink.

"How about King Arthur and the Knights of the Round Table," Conrad suggests. There's a collective groan. I feel them, but I hold mine in. I don't want to be like unsupportive.

"How about Cinderella," Colin counters.

Gigi claps her hands. "I love it. I can be Cinderella. I have the perfect dress."

"No," Kassidy replies, surprising us all. She's killer with graphics and design, but she's a bit of an introvert.

"No?"

"We should do like a whole Shrek and Fiona theme.

That would be so boss."

"You want us all to look like ogres," Gigi grumps.

"No. Just two people," Kassidy replies cheerily. "The rest of us can be like Donkey or Gingie."

"Don't forget the Three Blind Mice," Colin pops off.

Conrad snaps his fingers and points at Colin. "Shades," he says. "I'm in."

"Well, then. I guess that's decided. We will have a Shrek and Fiona themed carnival," Gigi says in a defeated tone of voice.

"It's going to be fun, Gigi. You'll see," Kassidy promises, and I believe her. When she makes up her mind about something, it gets done. And it is Boss.

Conrad does a table tap. "Is that it then? Are we done for the day?" He looks down at his phone.

Gigi gives him a glare. "Why? You got somewhere else you need to be?"

"Maybe."

"If it's alright with you, Gigi, I make a motion that we dismiss," I say in a submissive tone as possible.

"I second the motion," Colin blurts. Conrad tenses beside me.

"All in favor of adjourning the meeting say *aye*," Gigi orders. They all obey.

"All opposed?" The room is silent. "That's it then."

We get up and walk out. "What's your deal?" I say to Conrad as soon as we're in the hallway.

He grabs my hand and tugs. "Hurry up. This way," he whispers as we power walk in the opposite direction of everyone else.

I have no idea where we're going, but I'm not about to ask. We stand outside the library. He looks both ways before running his hand over the bottom of the fire alarm and pulling out a key. We enter the library. It's creepy and weird. No one else is here. It's all dark. "What are we doing?" I whisper.

"Looking for Meagan's mother."

What the heck? "She's not in here."

"Microfiche, Susan. Keep up," he scolds.

I do not like it. "Well, excuse me for not being all nosey."

"Don't worry. I will teach you my sleuthing ways," he jokes. I think. "What we're going to do is start scanning newspapers from whatever year she came to live with you and then like five years before that."

"And we can't google it because?" I ask.

"Because if there's something hidden on the level that I think it might be on, they're not going to make it easy to find."

"Who?"

"Whoever is hiding her."

I'm so confused. "What are you saying?"

"I'm saying she could be in the Witness Protection Program, and if she is, the government is going to do their best to keep her information off social media."

"Have you googled her real name?"

"Um, no, and I'm not going to. Did you?"

"No. I was going to wait to do it with you."

"I'm glad you did. I'm not googling her. I don't know who monitors what we search."

I give him a shove. "You sound a little paranoid."

He nods. "Better paranoid and safe than aware and dead."

I shiver at the thought. "That got dark fast."

He stops rolling the screen on the computer. "I'm giving her the benefit of the doubt, okay. But I'm telling you. If she changed her names and separated herself from her only daughter, then it's something major, and it's not gonna be good."

I scoot closer to him. The dark, empty room closes in on me, along with everything he just said. "Keep looking," I prompt as I sneak my hand between his arm and the rest of him and lean on his shoulder.

"Are you cold?"

No. At least not in the way he's thinking. "I'm feeling a little chilly."

I stare so hard at the screen my eyes burn. I hear a doorknob turn. He's out of his chair. He grabs my hand and yanks. I hear laughter. "Dude, are you sure it's in here?"

"Yeah, man. I left it in the history section."

Their footsteps get louder and louder. Conrad bumps me into a bookshelf. It wobbles. "I'm sorry," he mouths in my ear.

"Sorry for wha—" I say, and then he's kissing me. The back of my shirt is in his hands. He's kind of squishing me.

"Someone's rockin' the shelves," a guy says in a very suggestive tone. This is so embarrassing.

126

"Hey," he sort of yells, but Conrad acts like he doesn't hear him. I didn't think he could get any closer to me. We're already plastered to each other. His hands are in my back pockets. I resist the urge to pinch him. "Hey."

Conrad slowly inches his lips from mine. Just enough to turn in this guy's direction, but his hands stay where they are. Firmly planted on my butt. "Yeah, what?"

"What're you doing?"

"What's it look like I'm doing?" Conrad says all cocky like to Kevin, the scary senior who is well known for distributing any kind of illegal substance there is. This is so weird.

"Gettin' it on," Kevin says. He takes a step closer.

"Hey," Conrad yells back in the same way the guy did earlier. "Get your stuff and get outta here."

Small, wiry Kevin smirks. "Or what?"

"Whatever we're doin' is a lot less trouble than what you will be in," I challenge. I'm about to pee myself. Everyone says Kevin's half crazy. They also say he carries a knife that looks more like a dagger. I don't want to know.

Kevin's smirk turns to a frown. He steps a whole lot closer. "Don't be threatening me unless you can do something about it."

Conrad's hands fly about my back pockets. He steps in front of me. "If you don't graduate, you won't get that hot car your uncle promised you," he states.

"Why wouldn't I graduate?"

"If you get in-school-suspension too many times, they'll make you do summer school. I know a guy like you doesn't do summer school."

"No one's giving me ISS," Kevin says, but he sounds a little less sure of himself.

"I work in the office, Kevin. I'm not someone you want to mess with. I change records all the time," Conrad replies. He's totally lying out his butt.

Kevin stares at Conrad. Conrad stares right back. "C'mon man. He's not worth ISS or summer school. Let's go get lit," the other guy whines from somewhere across the room.

Kevin backs away. He points at Conrad. "We're not done yet. I got my eye on you."

Conrad puffs out his chest. "Same goes for me."

I lay a hand on the back of his arm as soon as Kevin disappears. Neither of us says a word until we hear the door close. "You're fricking crazy," I whisper.

"Certifiably," he replies.

He turns to look at me. "I'm sorry about all that. I didn't know what to do. Kissing you seemed the easiest explanation for why we're here."

"I get it. I mean, that's much better than him finding out what we were really doing."

"Yep." He walks back and sits in the chair in front of the computer. I sit down beside him. I wonder if his heart races like mine. "Not that I regret it," he adds. "It's just, it felt a little forced, you know. Like not at all like me."

"Really?"

He turns to look at me. His face inches toward me so slowly I don't notice him moving, but then his breath mixes with mine. "Really," he says before kissing me again, but this time it's different. It's slow and sweet. There's no rush. His hand grips my knee, but it stays there. It's all so wonderful. I want this moment to last forever. But we have to help Meagan. I can't believe how selfish I'm being. What am I doing sitting here making out with Conrad when her life could be in danger? I pull away. "I'm sorry. We have to help Meagan."

"You mean Mary."

"Whatever. She'll always be Meagan to me."

He scrolls and scrolls. Our eyes dart over the headlines. It feels like we could sit here for days. I can't believe we thought we'd just walk in and it would be right there. "What is Padrick doing?" I ask.

"What," he answers absentmindedly.

"Right now. What is your brother doing?"

"He's in chess club. Why?"

"I was just wondering how much time we have before we have

to get out of here. I don't want to like be locked in the school building overnight."

He laughs. "That would not happen. And if it did, I know how to get out of here."

"Do I want to know how you know that?" I tease, but I'm only half joking. There's more mystery to Conrad than I want to know.

"I'm the type of person who needs to be prepared. For everything. It's what keeps me calm. So, if there were to be like a school shooter situation, I need to know how to escape."

"Oh." I knew I didn't want to know.

"That's how I know."

"That makes sense."

"I know," he says in his matter-of-fact tone before continuing to scroll. "Aha," he says.

"What."

He points at the screen. "There. There it is."

The writing is so small. I don't know how he saw it. "She was a witness to a murder," I say as I read the fine print. "Her testimony put someone behind bars." I turn to look at him. "What's the big deal about that? People do it all the time. They don't have to disappear."

"It's *who* she put behind bars, Susan. That's where the problem is." I feel so clueless. How did he figure this out so quickly?

"Who was it?"

"I'm guessing the guy was mafia."

I think I'm going to be sick. "Are you serious?"

"Yeah. Either that or like a drug lord, but I'm betting mafia, because drug lords just kill everyone. They don't do ransom or hostage situations or wait someone out. That's mafia. They're in it for the long haul."

"What part of that is supposed to make me feel better?" I squeak. All I can think of is whoever has Meagan.

"Obviously they want her cooperation. That's why they took her daughter. Maybe this guy is up for parole and they're trying to get the mom not to talk."

My brain hurts. "What are you talking about?"

"Sometimes the prison system releases a person early on good behavior. The only way for them not to release the guy is if the victim's family or someone who can vouch for the person's character and why they should not be released early shows up and speaks on behalf of the victim. Sometimes it's a witness to the crime they committed."

"How do you know all this?"

He sighs. "My grandma works for the state. She contacts family's victims when the criminal is up for any kind of hearing. And my uncle is a lawyer. I hear things now and then."

"You're saying if Meagan's mom goes to this hearing to tell the Judge why the man should stay in jail, something bad will happen to Meagan."

"Hypothetically speaking, yes. That's my best guess."

"Which means the man who has her must be linked to the guy in jail."

"For all we know the bad guys are threatening him, too. Maybe he doesn't want to be a part of this, but he has to be."

This is so complicated and strange. "It's like a giant spider web," I muse.

He nods his head. "Exactly. We're all like a bunch of oblivious flies waiting to be caught."

I wrinkle my nose. "That's kind of gross. What do we do?"

"We tell Meagan her mom is alive."

"Wait, what? That's a terrible idea."

"I don't think we have another choice. We aren't going after this guy or his family. We can't go to the authorities."

"Why not?"

"I need to look further into this guy they put away. If there's any chance there were crooked cops involved, we can't chance telling them what we know."

I'm so lost right now. "Why do you think there would there be crooked cops?"

"Obviously there's a leak somewhere. Think about it. The guy who took Meagan knows about the release date. He also knows how to contact her mom who is supposedly being successfully hidden by the Witness Protection Program. There has to be a mole. That's what I'm saying."

"This is crazy. We're crazy. What are we doing?" It all catches up to me. I sound hysterical, but I can't help it. I can't believe Meagan is somehow tied to the mafia, or that my dad knew it all along. But he had to of. There's no way he had that in his desk drawer unless he knew. Unless Mom knows and she put it there. I'm losing it. "Do you think my mom knew?" I ask.

"It was in your dad's study."

"Yeah, but she's always been like the defender of Meagan. Like my dad didn't want Meagan around from the very beginning. He made that very clear, but Mom can be so stubborn."

"She thought she was helping Meagan, right?" Conrad asks.

Dad's words have me all confused. Why would he say my mother was just doing all that to look good? She wouldn't put our family at risk for the sake of appearances, would she? There's plenty of other things she could have done. Like start a charity or get involved with a humanitarian project. Serve at a soup kitchen. "Yeah. She was helping my friend," I answer, but my mind is all over the place. "For the sake of argument, if she knew but my dad didn't…" I pause. "Except that he *has to know*. I mean, I can't imagine my dad being okay with having a locked drawer in his desk that he can't get into. He just wouldn't allow it."

"What we don't know is if your mom and dad both know, or just your dad."

"And now us," I correct him.

"Well, yeah. Now us."

Our shared admission feels so intimate. This is so weird. "You got the guy's name and her real name, and we can leave." The library is creeping me out. This whole situation is creeping me out. I need some daylight. I don't like the dark.

———

I turn and wave at Conrad and Padrick backing out of the driveway before sneaking in the back door, trying not to make any noise. I'm not ready to face Mom and Dad after thinking about how much they might know and didn't tell me.

My phone vibrates. I look down.

RYAN:

I can't believe you're running around with
Conrad.

I read it twice. I can't believe my heart doesn't race like it used
to just a few days ago. Am I bi-polar? I can't believe I got over him
so quickly. But he let me go as soon as his dad told him to. So.

SUSAN:

I don't have time for this.

I send the Snap and feel so grown up, which is just so dumb.

"I can't believe this. He's your cousin. How could you not
tell me?"

Dad's voice makes me jump. I sneak up the rest of the hallway
and peek around the corner as much as I dare. His office door is
closed. I stay where I am, listening. "Why are you talking so
quiet," Mom demands. "It's not like anyone is here."

"Fine, Nell," Dad yells. "Is this better?"

I can't believe what's going on. I should say something.
Anything. To stop my parent's marriage from falling apart
completely. But I have to know what they're talking about. "Yes,
he's my cousin. Yes, he's family, but that's not my fault. I can't
choose family. You know this."

"Did you know this from the beginning?"

What the heck is going on?

Mom groans. "Are you seriously asking me if I knew when we
took Meagan in that she was going to end up being kidnapped by
my sketchy cousin who somehow has ties to the mafia? Is that
what you are saying?" Her voice is shrill. "And how could you not
tell me that her mom was in Witness Protection all this time?"

"My silence was part of the deal, Nell."

"Oh, that's terrific. You get to choose what you know that
you're keeping from me, but I can't do the same."

"I did it for the money."

"Excuse me?"

"*Money.* Why else would I do anything? You know we needed

132

the money. I'm not a game player." *Whatever, Dad. Sounds to me like you're pretty good at keeping secrets.*

"But my brother gave us the money."

"It may not look like it to you, Nell, but I'm still a man," Dad hollers. I blush clean through. *Mom doesn't emasculate him. Any feelings of inadequacy he has are his own fault.* Geez. What the heck is wrong with me, and why can't I shut off Meagan's voice inside my head?

"What does that mean?" she replies.

"Exactly," he says, and my heart breaks. I don't want to hear any of this anymore, but I can't walk away.

"I don't know what you are saying."

"Yes, your brother gave us money, but it wasn't enough. And I hated owing him anything."

"So you just went out and found somebody needing something in the worst way and you took advantage of it," Mom accuses, and I realize something. I am my father's daughter. No matter how I paint this picture of Meagan and I, I knew she needed me in the worst way, and somehow I managed to take advantage of our friendship, and she still ended up in the river. I'm a monster.

"I knew a guy, okay. I told him I was looking for a large amount of money, but I wanted to be legit about it. He told me he knew a mom needing to hide her daughter because they were in the Witness Program. He told me we wouldn't be in any danger. He told me I would be paid a decent amount. She was the same age as Susan. I had no idea what kind of girl we were going to get."

Mom sniffs. "You wanted a trouble-free girl with a big price tag attached who would benefit you."

There's a big noise. I think Dad hit the desk. "Don't *fricking* play that card with me, Nell. *You're* the one who wants to live in this neighborhood, and drive a new car, and have our daughter live in *this school district*. Don't you dare put this all on me. I didn't plan on losing my job I've had for twelve years because our company outsourced to some place in a third world country so our CEOs could keep their salaries while screwing management and everybody else over."

"Okay, okay. Please don't start that rant again. I've heard it so many times. That part of your life is done."

"Fine. I'm just saying I had no idea what a nightmare of a girl she was going to be. She's ruined our daughter's life, and all you did is stand by and watch. You'd walk through hell and back to accommodate our foster child while you leave our own daughter out in the cold."

"I do the best I can, Jeff. And you know that. I work. I come home, clean house, and make supper. I take the girls to all their appointments. I handle our checkbook. It's *all* on me. All you do is sit here in your tiny office doing goodness knows what on your computer all day. I'm the one handling everything."

My head hurts. I can't take much more of this. I hate Meagan all over again. How can one person cause so much pain and not even care? I can't believe Mom's cousin kidnapped Meagan. I can't believe my dad took a bunch of money.

"You paid my brother back, right?"

"Seriously, Nell? You think I wouldn't pay him back? Of course, I did. That's the first thing I did. I don't want to owe him anything."

"Did he ask how you got it?" Mom's voice is small again. I hate that she reduces herself to nothing to appease my father.

"No, and I didn't tell him. Your brother doesn't need to know everything about my life."

"Is this the reason you've been buying guns?"

"Maybe."

What is going on? Mom hates guns, and I thought Dad did too. Meagan has turned us all against each other. So why do I still miss her? Why do I worry about where she's sleeping or if she has enough to eat?

"What happens now?" Finally. Mom asks a question I want the answer to.

"We wait." Dad's cryptic answer fills me with dread. It's so strange. "Where's Susan?"

Oh, crap. "She's at school with Conrad. They had a yearbook meeting."

"That's good. At least she's focusing on something normal," Dad says.

"Yeah, but it's getting late. Maybe I should call her," mom says.

I rush down the hallway and out the front door. I come back in and let it slam behind me. "I'm home," I yell.

Mom comes around the corner, smiling. I shove everything I just heard from my brain, along with the reality that Meagan has been gone for almost five days. "Hey, Mom."

"Hi, honey. I saved you a supper plate. It's in the kitchen. You want me to warm it up for you?"

I'm not hungry. I'm not anything. I open my mouth to agree, but she looks so tired. "Thanks, but I can get it. Why don't you go hop in the bath with a glass of wine?"

She gives me a funny look. "Kerin says you need more downtime," I throw in there, because she kind of does. Really what she said was for me to stop being so mean to Mom all the time and try to walk in her shoes for once. At which point I told Kerin *no one walks in Mom's shoes because she makes sure they're too big for anyone to fill but her,* and then I immediately felt remorse for opening my mouth and popping off before thinking. Mom loves me. She has the best intentions, but she's only human.

"Okay. Maybe I will," she says.

I hurry to the kitchen to warm up my plate of food I probably won't eat. I need to get upstairs so I can Snap Conrad. I can't talk to him, because I don't want Mom or Dad to hear me. Minutes later I'm back in my room.

SUSAN:

Hey.

CO:

Hey. 🤍

I don't know if I can take a guy wearing his heart on his sleeve, but I don't want it to stop. It's adorable. I send a heart back and close my eyes for half a second. This is so weird. I've never sent one before.

SUSAN:

Got a minute?

CO:

For you? Always.

I roll my eyes. He's so cheesy.

SUSAN:

I found out more big news.

CO:

Oh. I thought this was a you and me convo.

I'm the worst girlfriend.

SUSAN:

I'm sorry. This is important.

CO:

Fine. I'll put away my flirty eyes and put on my P.I. cap.

I giggle. I can't help it.

SUSAN:

Mom's cousin has Meagan.

CO:

What? When?

SUSAN:

Now.

CO:

Does Meagan know who he is?

SUSAN:

IDK.

CO:

Do you know why? Is he connected? R U connected? I was just kidding when I said u were a criminal.

SUSAN:

No. I'm not connected. Geez.

CO:

Sorry. Proceed.

SUSAN:

He's into the M for something. I guess he owes them?

CO:

I called it.

SUSAN:

You did.

CO:

I am awesome.

SUSAN:

Get over yourself.

CO:

Is that it? Can we get back to you and me?

I'm warm from my toes to my nose. I swear. This boy.

SUSAN:

No. There's more.

CO:

What could be bigger than that?

SUSAN:

Do you want to know?

CO:

Yeah.

SUSAN:

You were right about the other hypothesis about why the mom is in hiding and still alive.

CO:

You mean she is innocent?

SUSAN:

As a bystander? Yes.

CO:

Got it. Say no more.

This feels so spyish. He doesn't want me to say the words, and I don't want to say them. We are so on the same wavelength.

CO:

I'm coming over.

SUSAN:

Now?

CO:

Yeah.

SUSAN:

But it's late.

No response. I start to type wear your reflectors but stop. My boyfriend isn't in elementary school.

I eat a few vegetables and a bite of chicken. Mom makes the best stirfry. I wish I were in the mood to eat it. Someone knocks at my window. Is Meagan back? I turn to see Conrad's smiling face. Why isn't he coming in? I go over and open the window. "You could have opened it."

He looks uncertain. "I didn't think I should enter without your permission."

I giggle. I can't help it. "You're definitely not Meagan," I say. He steps a lot closer, leans in, and kisses me. It's so hot.

It's a little bit before I back away. "What was that?" I tease, but I'm a little breathless. He looks too satisfied to not have noticed.

"I've always wanted to do that," he explains.

I giggle again. "Crawl through a girl's window and kiss her?"

His eyes go to the floor. He shoves his hands in his pockets. "Not just any girl," he answers.

"Good save," I joke.

He grabs my hand and holds on. "I meant what I said," he scolds.

I feel terrible. "I know," I say before sitting down on a chair.

He eyes my dinner plate. "You need to eat more," he states.

"Okay?"

He hands my plate to me. "Go on. I can wait."

I don't like him watching me. "Fine, but don't stare. I don't like eating alone."

He reaches over and grabs a green bean and pops it in his mouth. "There."

"But you hate green beans," I tell him before taking a bite of chicken.

"You make them less sucky," he answers, and I forget that I hate eating in front of my boyfriend.

"She's in the Witness Protection Program," I tell him between bites.

"And your dad took money for this," he confirms.

"Whisper," I say. "Your voice carries more than you think."

"Sorry," he whispers back.

"Well, it's complicated. My dad lost his management job because the company he worked for outsourced. So he had to borrow money from my mom's brother so they wouldn't lose the house, but you know how men are. They don't like to depend on other men, so he told his friend he needed some money, but in a legit way. His friend told him about this mom needing to find a safe place for her daughter who was my age, so he took the deal. They gave him a bunch of money. He paid off my uncle and then he paid whatever other amount of money he had to pay for us to stay here and live how we live," I say, feeling more than slightly embarrassed.

"Whoa. That had to be like a boatload of money."

"Yeah," I say, feeling not at all proud. "I guess Mom didn't know because he didn't tell her. She just found out."

"Kind of like he found out your mom's cousin is connected to the mafia, and he has Meagan."

I almost choke on my last bite of chicken. "Yeah, pretty much."

He goes to my mini fridge. "Can I have a drink?"

I nod. He opens it and takes out the last espresso. They were Meagan's favorite. That's why I haven't thrown it out. I don't want him to drink it. It's so stupid. I could buy another one, but then it wouldn't be hers. "Could you drink something else?" I blurt as he gets ready to pop the tab.

He stops moving. "Yeah," he says all casual like, but I can tell he's hurt.

"That was hers," I explain.

"Oh, right," he says in a disgusted tone of voice, and I completely agree, but I can't stop myself from wanting him to leave it alone. He grabs a can of Coke instead. "Can I have this one?" he asks, but there's a bit of sarcasm in there.

"Yeah," I answer, even though I don't think he's listening, considering he's already chugging it.

"If he's your mom's cousin, has she been in contact with him?"

I can't believe I didn't think of that. "I have no idea."

"Because they don't know that you know what they know," he supplies. "The parents," he adds.

"Yeah. Caught that, and pretty much."

He sits his butt on the floor near my foot and leans back on my leg. I never knew Conrad was so cozy, or that I would like it so much. Ryan didn't like physical contact unless it was going somewhere. I blush at the thought. I can't believe I'm comparing the two of them in my head.

"So we don't know how close any of this is coming to being over."

"No."

My brain hurts. I can't believe I'm about to do what I swore I never would do, but he knows about it anyways. I open the desk drawer and pull out the diary, which I kind of drop in his lap. "Open it to the first page," I say.

I watch him read over the rules of Crack-It. He tilts his head backwards to look up at me. "This is like really dark for a twelve-year-old girl."

I nod my head. "Yeah, but she wasn't your average twelve-year-old."

He laughs. "Yeah, but you still signed it."

I take a long drink of water from my straw. "Well, she was my friend. And it was a pact between us. I thought it was cool."

He lays the diary on the floor. "I guess."

"Do you think she's still playing?" I ask, even though I hate myself for saying it.

"She said she wasn't," he answers.

"I know, but it's so hard to forget all the games she played up until now."

He clears his throat. "If I had to guess, I would say she found out about her mom being alive, and she tried to find them on her own."

"And all this happened as a result," I say.

"Yep."

"And now she's stuck in the middle of the mess she created with no way out."

"Yep."

"So we should contact the police."

"Yep," he starts. "No. Wait a minute. We should definitely not do that."

"This is over our heads, Co. We can't solve this. It's too much."

"We already discussed this, Susan. We can't go to the police. We don't know how deep this goes," he argues.

"I don't want anyone else getting hurt," I argue.

"We have to tell your parents what we know," he says.

I tug at a hair on the top of his head. "Are you saying I should tell them I know what they know because I'm a snoop?"

He nods. "You have to."

"They're going to ground me."

He laughs. "Maybe that would be good for you. Then you can't get into any more trouble."

"Then I can't see you."

He wraps a hot hand around my ankle. "You'll still see me at school and school functions." He tips his head backwards again. I lean over and kiss him upside down. "I'm so cool. I'm Spider Man," he jokes before turning a little sideways. "You ate everything. Thank you."

I lay my empty plate on the desk. "Well, if I'm gonna fight with Mom and Dad, it better not be on an empty stomach." I look toward the window. "Guess you better go."

His hold on my ankle tightens just a little. "No can do, soldier. You can't go out on the battlefield alone."

I giggle. "Alright."

He gets to his knees, turns around and lays a hand on each side of my hips where I sit on the chair. "What are you doing?" I ask, but I already know, which is probably why I'm all excited.

"If I'm gonna get yelled at for crawling in your window, I may as well make it worth my time," he warns before kissing me senseless. I can't believe Conrad Banks is so hot. He hides it so well.

Minutes later, he backs off, mostly. His hands grip the sides of my chair. My hands rest on his shoulders. I can't stop staring. "You surprise me," I say. "You keep doing that."

He gives me a wink. "That's the idea."

He gets to his feet. "Come on, comrade. Let's go to war."

I grab my plate. We walk as quiet as two men sneaking in behind enemy lines. I step a little harder on the stair. I have no idea where my parents are or what they're doing. We find them sitting together on the couch, staring at a black TV screen. Weird.

"Co," Mom says a little too loud. "How nice to see you."

Dad frowns. "He didn't come in the front door."

I blush.

"No, sir. I didn't. I crawled in her window," Conrad answers. "But we have more important things to discuss."

Dad's face turns red. "Like what?"

I jog to the kitchen to set down my plate before returning in the same way. "We know, Dad. We know everything," I say.

"What does that mean?"

"We saw the birth certificate. We know about the money. We know Meagan's real name. We know her mother is alive. We know where Meagan is. We know who took her. We know why," Conrad rattles off.

Their jaws drop. I don't know how mine didn't. I thought he would have been smoother than that with his delivery. "How do you…" Dad begins.

I wave my hands in the air. "It doesn't matter how. I know. He knows. We all have to work together to get this thing figured out."

"What is there to figure out?" Mom shrieks. Great. She's all hysterical again.

"How this is going to end peacefully," I say, feeling like I'm talking about some sort of compromise that any of us have control over. Which is just stupid. We totally don't.

"We need to come up with a plan that minimizes any potential danger," Conrad continues.

Dad grips the side of the couch. "I am not comfortable with the amount of information the two of you possess or how you came to get it."

I stare him down. "I'm not comfortable with you keeping secrets that impacted everyone here except for Conrad." I say before turning to look at Conrad. "Sorry."

He takes my hand. "I'm not. I didn't want this to happen like this, but I can't be sorry we're together."

Mom blinks. "Just how together are you?" she asks. I want to fall through the floor.

"It's not like that," I say. I can't believe I'm answering this sort of question to my mother about my boyfriend in front of him.

"I'm a responsible person, Mrs. Tripp," Conrad answers.

I want to die. Not literally. But seriously.

"Can we talk about the plan?" I plead.

"Have you been contacting your cousin?" Conrad asks Mom.

She doesn't answer. Great. That tells me everything. "Since when?" I demand.

"When were you going to tell me Meagan crawled in your window, or that you threw her off a bridge?" Mom yells.

143

"I was being held at gunpoint," I answer back.

Dad turns on Mom. "Your freaking cousin held our daughter at gunpoint, and you didn't have a problem with that?"

"The gun wasn't loaded," Mom supplies.

"She didn't know that!" Dad roars.

"She's in *counseling*, Jeff," Mom shrieks.

"Because of your stupid family."

"If you hadn't taken the money and Meagan, none of this would have happened in the first place," Mom cries.

"She's right," Conrad agrees.

I take my hand from his. "You shut up," I bark, and then I immediately feel terrible. "I'm sorry, Co. I didn't mean it."

"I know you didn't, but that was really hurtful."

I keep my mouth closed. I don't want to say the wrong thing. I don't want him to leave. "I'm a big girl. I won't break," I say right before I burst into tears. "We have to save her. I can't take it if something happens to Meagan. It's not her fault," I bawl.

Conrad hands me a box of tissues. I turn away from him to wipe my face. I'm a big snotty mess.

"Jeff, you need to contact your guy, and Nell, you need to contact your cousin," Co orders.

"What guy?"

"The guy who found the source of money for you to begin with," Conrad explains.

"I can't."

Mom shoves her foot into the side of Dad's leg. "Oh, sure, Jeff. Make me feel terrible for contacting my cousin when I'm only trying to make sure Meagan is okay, but when we need you to cooperate for the good of the group, you refuse."

"I can't contact him because he's dead."

Mom sniffs. "I'm so sorry."

"How did he die?" Co asks.

I'm so stupid. How do I not pick up on these things?

"What do you mean?"

"Was it an accident or foul play?"

"It was a car accident. It caught fire."

"Are you sure?"

"That's what the news headlines said," Dad argues.

"That's what they wanted everyone to think," Co corrects him.

"What are you? Some sort of conspiracy theorist?" Dad demands.

"No. I'm a PI in training using logical, deductive reasoning. You yourself said the mom is in the Witness Protection Program. Maybe this man knew too much. Or maybe they found out who he was and that he was tied to Meagan and so they tried to make him talk and he wouldn't."

"Kid, you have some kind of imagination."

"You better hope he's wrong, Jeff, or they'll be coming for us next," Mom mutters.

"I can't go into hiding. I have homework," Co says, and I resist the urge to bust out laughing at the mention of his schoolwork in the middle of a serious crime involving murder. His words come back to me. "Did Meagan reach out to your cousin, or did he take her?"

Mom kicks at the floor. "She found out her mother was alive, and she went looking for her. He took her to try to keep her quiet and safe."

I wave my hands in the air. "I don't understand how your cousin has Meagan when Dad was the only person who knew her mother was in the Witness Protection Program."

Mom's hand goes to her head like she has a headache. "It was all a lucky coincidence I guess."

Conrad snorts. "There are no lucky coincidences when it comes to the mafia."

Dad stomps his foot. "None of that matters now. We are in it deep, and we have to find a solution."

"So this has nothing to do with a guy coming up for parole," Conrad prods.

"Well, that part is in there too," Dad agrees. "It was all very bad timing."

"Like Murphy's law," Conrad supplies.

"Something like that," Mom murmurs.

Dad's eyes narrow on Conrad. "How do you know all this if you're not involved?"

I get between Conrad and Dad. "When this all went down with Meagan, I paid him to be my PI We found the birth certificate in your desk drawer in the office. We went to the school library and found information about her mother in the newspapers on the microfiche. We know what she saw. We know the name of the guy in jail. We know he's coming up for parole."

"Basically, the guy in jail wants Meagan not to talk and he has something on Mom's cousin so he made him kidnap her so her parents won't show up for the parole hearing," Dad replies.

"That's about the size of it," Conrad answers.

"She's gone four years without seeing her daughter because she was an accidental witness to a crime, and now she's supposed to keep her mouth shut so she can have her back," I ask.

Dad nods his head. "I bet she will too. There's nothing I wouldn't do for you," he says as he looks up at me from where he sits on the couch. I wish I had more reassurance from his words, but given the mess we're in, it has the opposite effect.

"If she wants Meagan back, her mother has to go against everything she believes in, and not do the right thing," I argue. "Do you think she will?"

Mom looks the other way. "It's like Dad said. There's nothing parents won't do for their children."

My stomach hurts. I hope my supper doesn't come back up.

"What are you going to tell your kidnapper cousin?" Conrad asks Mom.

She looks so helpless sitting there. "I don't know."

"How do you know where her mom is?" Dad cuts in.

"I don't," Conrad says.

"You said you did."

"I didn't mean it like that. I was just saying we know she isn't dead," Co replies.

"Oh."

I study Dad and Mom. "You guys don't know where she is?"

They shake their heads. "No, dear. That's why they call it the Witness Protection Program."

Dad's hand bounces against the arm of the couch. "I say Conrad goes home and we all sleep on it."

That sounds like a great idea to me, except for one thing. For every day that goes by, Meagan is somewhere out there with her captor. Alone and afraid. "But Dad, tomorrow is day five. It's almost been a week since she left."

"I know, sweet pea. But the bad guy's not up for parole until the day after tomorrow, so we still have one more day to figure this thing out. Everyone's tired. We aren't thinking clearly." He tilts his head to the side. "I didn't hear your car pull in."

"I rode my bike, sir," Co answers.

Dad smirks. "You rode your bike," he repeats in an amused tone that suggests Conrad has training wheels.

"I'm fourteen, sir. To drive a car would be against the law," Co states. He fidgets. "I mean, I know how to drive a car, but you know, I'm not supposed to."

Mom nods her head. "That's very responsible of you."

Conrad wears a look of frustration. I know Mom didn't mean to, but I don't think he likes feeling placated.

Dad looks out the window. "It's awfully dark. How about I toss your bike in the truck and take you home?"

Panic fills Co's face for half a second. "Sure. Okay."

"I'm coming," I interject. There's no way I'm letting Dad drive Conrad home. I can only imagine what he's going to say.

"The more the merrier," Dad practically sings. This is going to be awful.

The ride to Conrad's house is a strange one. Dad turns on a station he never listens to and cranks the radio. The truck is still moving a little when Conrad hops out in his driveway. He runs to the back to lift his bike out. Dad starts to get out. "Maybe I should help him with his bike."

I grab his arm. "Please don't. He's got it," I say, and I hope he does. Dad's truck is a little high and Conrad's medium height. Things bump around a few times, but he gets it over the edge. I roll down my window. "See you later," I say.

Conrad waves from beneath the yard light he just set off. "See you," he says.

His house door opens. "Conrad, what are you doing out here?" his mom questions.

147

I turn to my Dad. "Can we go now?"

He grins at me. "This is just getting good."

"I went over to see my friend," Conrad explains. "And it's Co, I told you this."

"Girlfriend," Dad yells out my side window.

I punch him in the arm. "Shut up, please." This is so embarrassing.

"You have a girlfriend," his mom exclaims as she marches past him in her flannel jammy pants and slippers. She wears a hoodie. Her hand is over her eyes even though it's dark. Conrad stands somewhere behind her. Her hands rest on the truck window. "Hi, I'm Conrad's mom," she says.

I lean away from my dad. The light hits my face. Her expression of curiosity changes to a smile. "Oh, hey Susan. I know you." She waves her hand. "Silly me, I should have known. You're all my son talks about."

She turns to look back at Conrad. He hasn't moved from where he is, stuck somewhere between Dad's truck and his own front door.

"Is that right?" my dad booms from where he sits behind the steering wheel. "Susan hasn't said much about him, but I understand this is all sort of new."

This is so humiliating. Why can't we be normal? I paste on a smile and try to ignore Dad's giving me crap. "It's so nice to see you. We were going home. It's kind of late."

"Are you sure? Y'all could come in for some hot chocolate or tea," Conrad's mom offers.

Dad clears his throat. "That's so nice, but I think we're going to take a raincheck if you don't mind. I think the kids both have homework they're working on."

"Well, okay then. Y'all have a good night," she says before turning to walk toward Conrad. She slaps a hand on his back. "I really like her. She's a sensible girl."

Dad snorts beside me. I roll up the window as fast as I can. "Can we go now, please?" I beg. He backs up until he's on the road. He puts the truck in drive.

"Susan, don't you think you're robbing the cradle just a little with that boy?" he teases.

I'm so glad it's dark. I know he's joking, but it's embarrassing. Conrad has a tiny bit of a baby face. He can't help the shape of his face, but it makes him look younger than he is.

"Mom is three years older than you," I fire back.

He slaps the steering wheel. "Yep. I've always liked older women," he crows. I know he's kidding, but seriously. *Gross*. He's my dad.

"What do you think we should do to get out of this mess?" I ask.

He turns the radio down. "I don't know yet."

I wiggle in the seat beside him. "Conrad thinks we shouldn't go to the local police because he's worried they could be involved."

Dad frowns. I wish he would laugh or do something that shows he thinks Conrad's crazy. That would make me feel so much better. "He might be onto something," he answers. For once I wish Conrad was wrong.

"Oh," I say, because I don't know what else to say.

"Yeah, so, I'd have to find someone higher up maybe."

"How do you that?"

He makes a groaning noise as we turn into the driveway of our house. "I imagine I'd have to call your uncle, which I don't want to do, but he's got connections from being ex-military."

I catch movement on the roof. My heart races. Meagan must be back. I smack my forehead to distract my father in case he catches me looking up. "Oh, yeah. Duh. I can't believe I forgot Chris was in the army."

"The Rangers," dad says. "They're Special Forces." He taps his fingers on the wheel. "'Course now a bunch of them are Border Patrol. They spend their days chasing homeless people down."

"That's kind of sad," I say. "For everyone."

"Yep."

I open the door. "I'm just gonna go in. I think I might have a little homework, like you said." I jog inside, toss as much stir fry on my plate as I dare without drawing suspicion and head upstairs. Stir fry is Meagan's favorite.

I open my room door and close it again. There's no one in the room. There's no one at the window. I set the plate down on the desk and plop down in my chair. Someone rises from the floor on the other side of my bed. It's not Meagan. It's a man. I almost pee my pants. I glance at my closed door at the same time he does. His hands raise slowly. Thank God they're empty. "I'm alone," he says.

I'm so confused. "Who are you?"

"I lost her," he says.

"Meagan," I ask. "You lost my friend?"

He nods his head. "Don't tell me her name. Don't tell me anything about her. I don't want to know. I'm only doing what they tell me I have to do so I can see my family again."

"What happened?" I ask. "How did you lose her?"

"She attacked me."

I narrow my eyes. "What were you doing to her?"

His eyes widen. "Nothing. I swear. Things were going as well as they could go between us. I was being kind. I let my guard down for a split second, and she hit me in the side of the head with something, and then she took off." He looks around the room. "I thought she might come here."

I remember what Dad said about him being Mom's cousin. I look closer at him. "You look nothing like my mom," I say.

Confusion fills his face. "Okay?"

"It's just...you're family," I tell him.

"What about my family?" he asks.

"No. That's not what..." I stop mid-sentence. Mom's been talking to him, but she didn't tell him they're related. He doesn't know. What the heck is going on?

He stares at me. "I hope they're okay," I answer, and I mean it. If the bad guys find out he doesn't have Meagan, what will they do?

"Thank you," he says.

I don't know what to do. This is all so strange. I hold the plate out. "Would you like some food?"

He crosses the room and grabs it. "Thank you," he says as he crams the food in with his fingers, which is a bit gross, but I'm glad I kept the fork. It could be used as a weapon. "You want to give me your number?" I offer, surprising myself. I don't know why I'm asking. "In case she shows up here. I could tell you." He looks torn. "I don't know your family, but I'm sure they're very nice."

"Okay," he says, before rattling it off. I scribble it down in my notes in my phone and tag it *Meagan's guy*. This is so messed up. "Do you know where she might go?"

"I'm sorry. I don't," I say, wishing he would leave. "But if I think of something I'll let you know," I say. He sets the plate on my bed and crawls out the window. I breathe a little easier. His head pops back in, startling me. "I'm sorry I pulled that gun on you," he says.

I want to tell him it's no problem, but that's a lie. "Was it loaded?" I ask.

He gives me an incredulous look. "Why carry a gun if it's not," he answers.

I can't believe Mom lied to Dad about the gun. If Mom and this guy haven't been talking about Meagan, what were they talking about? He stares at me as if he's waiting for an answer. This is so weird. "Thanks for not shooting me," I say.

He nods. "I may have a gun, but that doesn't make me a murderer," he insists.

I'm not so sure. What would he have done if I refused to do what he said that night? "Well, I guess I'll see you later," I say. The doorknob on my door rattles. I panic. His eyes widen. He tugs the windowsill down and disappears. I whip around. Mom opens the door. She studies me. "You talking to someone?"

My head spins. "No."

"I thought I heard a guy's voice."

If she's been talking to her cousin, wouldn't she recognize his voice? We were speaking in muted tones, but still. "Huh. I don't know. I was just practicing forensics," I answer. I can't think of another reason to be talking out loud by myself. I think of what just happened. I wonder why he didn't tell Mom Meagan's missing again. What if she isn't? What if she sent him in here to tell me that to see what I would do? No, she wouldn't do that. Not when her mom's life is at stake. But she ran away from him knowing that might put them in danger. What does that mean? Where could she possibly be?

"Susan," Mom scolds.

"Yeah, what?"

"It's cold in here. You should really close that window," she says as she points.

He didn't close it all the way. "Oh, yeah, right. Sorry," I say as I hurry over to close it. My concentration is shot.

"Darling," Mom says in her sweet mother voice.

"Yeah," I answer.

"I'm going to take a bath. You try to get some rest. Dad's right. We're so tired. We can't think straight."

"Okay, Mom." *Yeah, right. I'm not getting any sleep. Meagan is on the loose. Who knows what she's doing.*

I change into my pajamas. I crawl beneath the covers. I stare at the ceiling for what feels like hours. Twenty-six minutes creep by as I steal glances at my digital alarm clock. I should get up and look for clues. Or do something other than lay here thinking I should do something but still not do it. I can't sleep, but there's no point in getting up. If I didn't find anything before now that gives me a clue of where Meagan is or what she's doing, I'm not going to.

Someone's shaking me. My hands fly out in defense. "Don't smack me," she says.

I'm wide awake. "Meagan?"

She sits on the side of my bed. "Hey."

I scoot up against my headboard. "Hey," I answer. I have no idea what's going on. I want to ask her why she's here, but I don't. It's just like old times. I'm waiting for her to tell me what to do, or what to say. I wonder how much she knows about the man she escaped from. I wonder if she knows what Mom and Dad know.

"I know my name," she says.

"You'll always be Meagan to me," I answer, even though it sounds dumb as soon as I say it.

She turns to look at me. There's so much emotion in her eyes I almost can't breathe. I've never seen her this way. She's lost. She's hurting. She's vulnerable. I hate myself for being so cruel. I hate my parents for keeping her in the dark. "All I want is my mom," she vows.

"You will, Meagan. You'll find her," I promise. I hope my words are true.

"My mom is gone, Susan. What are you saying?"

Oh crap. What have I done? "Why were you with him?"

She blinks. "I thought I was protecting you."

My heart pinches. "Oh."

"But then I heard him. Talking to your mom." Her head falls back. She looks at the ceiling. "I can't believe she betrayed me."

"She wanted to help you. You have to believe that."

Her gaze meets mine. Her eyes burn bright with anger. "Why would she be talking to the man who kidnapped me if she was trying to help me?"

That's a fair question. "I don't know."

She studies me long enough to be awkward, but that's nothing new. "You know something."

My fingers fidget in my lap. "Conrad and I have been working non-stop trying to find...trying to help you." I break her intense gaze and stare down at my lap. "I think there are things you know, too, but you're not telling me." If she's not looking for her mom, who is she looking for?

She lays down on the side of the bed. Her back is to me. "Can I sleep here? I'm so tired."

I turn on my side and put my back to her. "Yeah."

I stare into the shadows of the early morning hours. It's still dark outside. She didn't deny the last thing I said. Some things don't change, but some things do. For the first time since we've been friends, Meagan's not the only one keeping secrets.

15

DAY FIVE

Badge 343

"William."

Desire hits me hard and fast, like I'm sixteen-years-old all over again, but in my defense, her soft voice woke me out of a dead sleep. I wake on my side with one hand on my gun from the night-table drawer. An unmistakable scent fills my bedroom. It's more real than any dream I've ever had about her, and I've had plenty. My gun hand covers most of my chest. I close my eyes and lay my head back. "Marlena," I whisper her name somewhere between a curse and a prayer.

"You remember me," she taunts, as if she doesn't know she's the one woman I fantasized about for far too long, and the last person I thought would be breakin' into my home at four in the mornin'.

"You're kinda hard to forget," I reply. "What's goin' on?"

"I hear my daughter's gone missin'."

"And you don't know where she is?" I say out of disbelief and frustration. I'm so tired of losin' sleep over these O'Reilly women and their cryptic games.

"Would I be here if I did?" she counters.

"I don't know," I admit.

I hear footsteps, but they're so soft I can't tell where she's goin'. My ears stop strainin' when my King-sized mattress moves. I chuckle when she tugs on my comforter. This is the strangest day of my adult life.

"What's so funny?" she whispers near my ear, and I'm stiff as a board. Everywhere.

"That's the last thing I thought I'd hear a woman say who's lyin' beside me," I growl.

Her nose bumps my earlobe. I can't believe I forgot how cruel Marlena O'Reilly can be. Her hand clutches my gun. She slides it off my chest in super slow motion. Her inner wrist skims the skin of my chest. Her forehead bumps my chin. "I never took you for a whiner, *William*," she says. Her lips touch my jaw about the time her breath attaches itself to the side of my neck. I have no idea what's goin' on.

"I'm not a whiner," I protest.

"Are you gonna kiss me?" she asks. Her words burn my ears before settin' fire to the rest of me. All I have to do is turn my head, and my lips will touch hers. I'm frozen. I can't think. I can't move. I'm not sure I'm breathin'. The girl of my dreams showed up in my bed nine years too late.

"What about your daughter?" I manage.

"She's not here," she answers before her lips find mine. I've been waitin' for this moment for far too long; the moment Marlena O'Reilly becomes more than just my favorite daydream...and now here she is in the flesh, lyin' next to me in my bed, and all I can think as our lips meet, our breath mixes, and her soft curves fit just right, is her daughter is missin' and she's seducin' me. I allow myself one last second of unfettered madness before pushin' her away.

Her shirt is off. She's braless. I must be certifiably insane. "Put your shirt on, Marlena. We have to find Meagan. This is not the time for that."

She leans forward just enough for the moonlight to burn her

every perfection into my memory as she tugs the sweatshirt over her head with the speed of a sleepy sloth. "You're a good man, William," she teases.

"So they keep tellin' me," I mumble. "Do you have any idea where she is?" I ask.

"Would I be here if I did?" she replies, and I notice that's the second time she's answered my question with a question. If I were a bettin' man, I'd say she knows a lot more than she's lettin' on.

"If she's not here but you're not too worried about where she might be, I'd say there's a good chance you already know where she is," I accuse as I let go of what remains of Marlena O'Reilly, the hottest girl I thought I knew and wanted. "Did you come back for your daughter or someone else?" I say in a voice heavy with regret.

She smacks me playfully in the chest. "I see you finally caught your long, tall shadow. I gotta say it's sexy as hell." Her voice lowers. I fumble for the switch to the lamp, but then I stop. Some dreams are hard to let go.

"I wasn't talkin' about me."

Marlena lets out a long sigh that's so sexual in nature I almost forget what I'm after. "You're not gonna be distracted, are you, *lawman*?"

"Nope," I bark. I'm not sure I'm talkin' to her or certain parts of my betrayin' anatomy.

"Preacher was right. Coming here wasn't such a hot idea after all."

Hearin' his name come out of her mouth while she's in my bed throws cold water on whatever embers linger. "Preacher? What's he got to do with any of this?"

"A lot more than you think."

I roll off my side of the bed, bein' careful not to touch her. "Guess we better go see him then," I challenge.

"Now?"

"Yeah, now. He's a preacher. I'm sure he's taken more than one early mornin' phone call. He won't mind," I say with a forced smirk.

I think she hits my bed with her hand. "Well, it won't be the first time I drag him out of bed, and I'm sure it won't be the last."

She can't mean what I think she means. Preacher has a lot of flaws, but bein' a hypocrite ain't one of 'em. There's no way he's climbed into bed with Marlena O'Reilly, no matter how temptin' she might be, and she doesn't strike me as the type to call on the church for help. I turn away to step into my uniform, not because I'm on duty, it's just the closest thing to my bed.

"What, no holster?" she jokes right before I bend over and pick it up off the floor.

"You're stuck with me now, Marlena, until this thing is done. I'm takin' my gun."

I slide a hand through her arm as I walk beside her and mostly forget she's not wearin' a bra. "Do you know where he lives?"

I start at her question. "Of course I know where he lives. I'm the Sheriff."

She laughs out loud. "You're tellin' me you know every house in this town?"

Even though I know she's askin' for the impossible, it bugs me I can't fulfill it. "I know at least half," I offer as we walk out the front door. I turn my key in the lock. "How'd you get in my house?"

She ducks her head and smiles to herself. I catch a glimpse of the girl I once knew, the one that caught my attention, a quiet, insecure girl with her own secrets. "I have my ways," she replies in a way that brings up another question I'd forgotten about.

"Did you really hit Hammy Hamilton with a brick?"

If I'm not mistaken, Marlena has a little trouble breathin'. "Who told you that?"

"That's irrelevant. Is it true?"

"Don't you wanna know why?"

I bite the inside of my cheek. "I'm guessin' he forced himself on you."

Her hand grips the side of the seat. "Just because I had a reputation doesn't mean he could take what I didn't offer," she says in a voice so quiet, there's no mistaking her self-doubt. I want to shoot Hammy Hamilton in the head, disability and all.

"No, it does not," I bark, like an order.

She jumps in her seat. "Thank you," she says just as quiet.

"Is he the father?" I ask.

She turns to look at me. The whites of her eyes glow in the dark. "My daughter has no father," she says. "Better no father than a man like that."

I nod my head. "This is true." We take the scenic route to Preacher's house. She lays the seat all the way back. "Someone lookin' for you?" I ask.

She turns to me and smiles again. "They always are."

I give her shoulder a shove. "Some things never change."

She shrugs. "Don't park out front. Pull into the shed behind his house."

I do as she says. We walk up to the back door. "Turn around," she says to me.

"What? Why?"

"Just do it. I don't want you to see the key."

"Fine, but it's either under the mat, the flowerpot, or close to the doorbell."

The door shuts on the last word I say. I turn back around. She's not outside. I open the door.

"Why'd you bring him here?" Preacher asks.

I step into the next room. "Either you got up to go to the bathroom or you never went to sleep." His hair is all messy, but he's still wearin' jeans and a K-State sweatshirt. I swear he's got about twenty of 'em.

He runs his hand through his hair before pointin' at Marlena with a disgusted look on his face. "She's supposed to be hiding out here. The second I use the bathroom, she's out the door." He stares at the two of us. "I should have known she would run over to your place and crawl into your bed."

I'm so confused. Why does Preacher know her business, and why does it sound so personal? "Hold up, we never, I mean I don't have that kind of history with her," I say as if I'm confessin', even though I didn't do anythin' wrong. At least not with her.

"Exactly," he states.

I study Marlena, tryin' to figure her out. "Is that why you came over to my place? Was I just gonna be another notch in your bedpost?"

She hugs herself. "That's not why I came to you."

"But you took your shirt off," I protest.

"I don't like rejection," she argues.

Preacher's eyes widen. "You turned her down?"

I'm such an idiot. "I've had a lot on my mind lately, like the missin' girl. Marlena's daughter."

"Meagan? She's not missing."

What is goin' on? How does Preacher know so much, and I know so little? And why didn't he tell me before now? "Just because you're a man of God doesn't mean you can hide behind your pulpit."

He steps closer to me. "Do you see me hiding?"

His intensity surprises me. He has strong feelings for the O'Reilly girls. I wonder why. "What's the deal with you two?" I ask.

"What do you mean?"

"Just what I said. Are you like the father of her child or something? Is Meagan your daughter?"

He shakes his head back and forth. "Hardly. I'm..." he looks over at Marlena who stares at the floor. "I'm her uncle."

I search my brain for a logical explanation. Preacher has siblings but they're all brothers, and none of them are Meagan's father. "I don't understand."

"He's my brother," Marlena supplies.

Her mother's words ring in my ears. "But your mother said she was..." I stop when I see the pain in her eyes.

"Her mother was thirteen. My father was eighteen," Preacher answers.

My stomach churns at the thought. "She was in seventh grade." I state the obvious, but I don't know what else to say.

"Yep," Marlena agrees. "My mother was a child when she had me. Her mother tried to make her get rid of the pregnancy, but she refused. She ran off the first chance she got. She went to live with her aunt up north."

"But you went to school here."

She nods her head. "When I was three or four, Grandma O'Reilly came for us. See, Momma never told her who the father was. When Grandma caught wind of the local gossip, she was mad enough to kill Preacher's father. She came and got the two of us and took us back to the farm. Grandma told my mom it wasn't her fault. She told her there was nothin' to be ashamed of, and if he didn't like seein' his sins walkin' around, he could leave town."

"So you grew up knowin' who your father was?" I ask.

She shakes her head again. "No. Not really. That conversation between Mom and Grandma wasn't had in front of me." She nudges Preacher's foot with her toe. "Preacher here figured it out in high school. That's when he became a man of God, and that's when he started tryin' to change me. I can't say his preachin' took, but he's always been there for me. Like the brother I never had."

He frowns. "I *am* your brother, Marlena. You'll always be my family."

She laughs, and it's like old times. Everyone else is feeling as uncomfortable as a nun in a bar, and Marlena's havin' a good ole' time. "Pissed yer ole' man off, too. I'm the last person he wanted his son runnin' around with." She shoves her hands in her back pockets, rocks back on her heels, and sticks out her front. Her green eyes lock on mine. "Right before mom had me, Preacher's dad had already talked his other woman into a shotgun weddin' 'cause Preacher was also on the way. By the time his woman found out what her husband done to my mom, Preacher already had two little brothers and another on the way. There was nothin' his wife could do but stay with 'em."

"When I found out I had a sister, I didn't care what dad thought about us hanging out. I just wanted to know more about her," Preacher says all quiet like.

"I know."

"Do you know where Meagan is?" I interrupt. It's gettin' too heavy in here.

Marlena turns her back on Preacher to look at me. "She'll come out when she's ready. Meagan's always known how to hide."

So many responses hit my brain, but I keep my mouth shut

and remind myself for the hundredth time Marlena was raised by a survivor. She had teeth before she knew how to use them.

Even though I know that, and can excuse Marlena's poor parentin' on some level, one problem remains. Meagan is the third generation of feral humans. If she feels cornered, there's no tellin' what she might do.

16

wake to the sound of my phone buzzing. It's Conrad. "Hello," I say as I glance at the back of Meagan's head. She's still here. Sound asleep. I creep across the room toward my closet.

"He's dead."

"Excuse me?"

"The man. The man in jail. He's dead."

My heart races in my chest. "Are you sure?"

"Did you not see the article I sent you?"

"I'm sorry. I just woke up. I was up late. I couldn't sleep."

"That sucks."

"Yeah." I don't want to tell him, but I have to. "She came back. She's in my room."

"Who came back?"

I sigh. "Who do you think?"

"Meagan?"

"Yeah."

"Does she know the bad guy died? Wait, where's the guy who took her?"

I giggle nervously. "I guess she attacked him, and she escaped."

"Seriously?"

"Yeah. After we dropped you off, Dad and I went home. We were in the truck in the driveway. I saw someone on my roof. I thought it was her, so I hurried inside and grabbed some food in the kitchen and went upstairs. Stir fry is her favorite. I thought she'd be hungry."

"And then what?"

"Well, I went in my room and closed the door in case she was like there."

"But she wasn't?"

"No. It was him. The guy who took her."

"He was in your room?"

"Yeah. He scared the crap out of me too. I like sat down on a chair because my room was empty, and so I thought I was wrong about someone climbing in my window, but then he like rose from behind my bed. It was so weird."

"He rose? Where he was he? On the floor?"

I nod my head again. "Yeah."

"Dude. That's super creepy."

"Thank you. I know."

"But if he was there, then how did she get there if they weren't together?"

"I don't know, but I have his number."

"What are you gonna do? Call him and tell him the guy is dead?"

"Maybe. He said he has a family, and he's just trying to keep them safe."

"Better call him now then," he says, and then he's gone.

I go to my notes for the random number and call it.

"Hello," he says.

"This is Susan from last night," I say. "The guy is dead. Someone in prison got him. I thought you better know."

"Are you sure?"

"Yes."

"This is very bad. I don't know what they'll do to my family."

"Call the Preacher," her voice sneaks around the door and cuts into my conversation.

"I'm so sorry," I say to the man on the phone. "I have to go."

"Don't call him," he says, I think. I'm not sure. I hang up the phone. I don't want to know why he said that, but things must be bad if Meagan is telling me to call the Preacher.

I hang up the phone. "I don't know his number," I say to her.

She rattles one off. My fingers shake as they dial the number. It rings three times. "Hello."

"Is this Preacher?" I ask.

"Yes."

"This is Susan Tripp. Meagan told me to call you."

"Is she alright?" He sounds genuinely concerned.

"Yes. Um, I need to tell you that someone died."

"Who?"

I look over at Meagan. She's nodding her head. I guess that means Preacher already knows everything. "The man in jail. He died. Someone killed him."

"You're sure?"

I consider my source. "My friend told me it was in the news just today. You can check if you want to."

"Sheriff," the Preacher says. "The inmate is dead. Someone got to him. Meagan is with a girl named Susan."

"Susan," Sheriff Chatham's voice is on the phone. *Crappity crap crap.* I ignore every instinct that tells me to end the call. Now.

"Yeah."

"Make sure Meagan stays with you."

Yeah, right. Like I can control any part of that statement. "Okay."

"I have to go back to him," she says.

"Who," I ask, although I think I already know.

"The man who kept me. If I don't go back to him, someone will hurt his family."

"But what if those people hurt you?" I reply.

"They won't so long as I'm with him." She's out of bed. She's at the window. What could I possibly say to make her stay?

"You know they killed him, Meagan. You know he's dead. He's not going to get out of prison. You can't go. You have to stay here. Nowhere else is safe."

"If I don't go back to him, I'll never see my mom again. That's what he said," she cries.

I'm so confused. "I thought you said your mom is gone."

"I thought she was, but he said she isn't. I thought he was just being cruel, but what if he isn't? What if my mother is alive?"

The hope and hurt in Meagan's eyes tears me in half. I'm the worst. Why didn't I tell her before her mother was alive? "She is, Meagan. She's alive."

"What? How do you know?"

"I found your birth certificate in Dad's study. Conrad and I looked her up. He found a picture of her sitting on a park bench. It was dated a month ago. She was a witness to a murder committed by a guy who is in the mafia. She testified. They had to put her in the Witness Protection Program. Somehow the mafia didn't know about you. She wanted to keep it that way, so she left you with my parents." I study her. "Wait a minute. If you didn't know your mom was alive, why did you take off with that man?"

Meagan looks all embarrassed as her gaze breaks and she looks at the floor. She shifts from one foot to the other. "A guy contacted me, okay? A guy I knew from junior high. I had a major crush on him. I thought I was meeting him, but it wasn't. It was my kidnapper."

This is so weird. "Was it J?"

Her eyes narrow. "Where'd you hear that name?"

I shrug. "You left pages of your diary in my closet. I found them when I was looking for clues. I thought you meant for me to see them."

Her fists clench at her sides. "Not really, but I guess what's done is done." She stares me down.

17

"S he's here," I say from the hallway. I feel like a real creeper standin' outside a room listenin' to two teenage girls talkin' in what they think is a private conversation, but these two have created quite the mess.

"Sheriff Chatham?" Meagan asks as she opens the door.

"Would you like to see your mother?"

A tear rolls down her cheek. "I would."

We walk downstairs together. Marlena flies across the room. She runs into Meagan so hard she almost tackles her. Marlena's arms fly around her, squeezin' her tight.

"I can't breathe," Meagan whines, but she sounds so happy. Preacher stands off to the side.

Susan hands me a piece of paper with a number on it. "This is the phone number for the guy who took Meagan," she says just as Mrs. Tripp's eyes widen in alarm. "I have to tell him, Mom," Susan says. "The rest of his family might be in danger."

"But we're his family," her mom blurts.

Meagan slips from her mom's grasp. "You know my kidnapper," she says to Mrs. Tripp.

"I do, but I didn't know he was related to me when you went missing," she says.

I dial the number. "Has anyone contacted you?" I ask him.

"No. Not yet."

"This is the Sheriff. Meagan and her mom are with me. Do you want to come downtown so we can talk?"

"I can't do that, Sheriff. If I do, I know I'll never see my family again," he says. I can't help but notice Mr. Tripp hangs on every word I say. He's more connected than he's admittin' to. It's just a hunch, but I'm a firm believer in intuition.

"I've got your number and quite a bit of technology at my disposal. It's only a matter of time before your cell phone pings off the cell towers. I will find you," I say. "It would be better for you if you turn yourself in."

"I'll think about it," he says, and then he hangs up.

Mrs. Tripp's lower lip quivers. "Is it true, Sheriff? Do you think the mafia will come after my family?"

"I can't believe you sent your cousin after my daughter," Marlena screams in Nell Tripp's face.

Jeff is on his feet. His finger almost touches Marlena's chest. "Don't you yell at my wife. Your daughter has been no end of trouble since the day she set foot in this house. My wife had nothing to do with the man who took your daughter. It was her own choice to go with him. Ask her."

Marlena turns back to Meagan. "Honey, is this true?"

"I thought he was someone else," she all but whispers. "I thought he was a guy who was my age. I was so tired of living here." She turns to glare at Jeff. "I know when I'm not wanted." She takes a deep breath. "And I know you took money to keep me. I never saw any of it, and I doubt I will. You're probably using it all on Susan's college. You could have given some to me."

Jeff's face darkens. "You're a nosey little brat. If I gave you that money you would just waste it. All you did was disrupt my household. We were all much happier before you came along."

Marlena hugs Meagan to her side. Nell takes Susan by the hand. They both move farther away from Jeff. This is turnin' out to be a terrible day. "I don't suppose you're gonna to give me any of the money either," Marlena says to Jeff.

"I can't. It's gone," he announces, but his eyes dart back and forth. He's lyin'.

"It was you, wasn't it," Meagan says so quiet, I almost don't hear her. She's starin' at Jeff. "You set this whole thing in motion. There was never any mafia involvement. There was never any threat."

He fidgets. He coughs. "I don't have to answer to you. You're just a girl," he spits back at her.

Nell clears her throat. "Maybe not, but you'll answer to me, husband. Is what she said true?"

He sniffs. "Obviously not. I got the money to keep her, didn't I? There was a definite need for protection. That's where her mother has been all this time."

Marlena crosses her arms on her chest. "I've been moved so many times. None of it was luxurious. Trust me, the Witness Protection Program is nothing like you see on TV."

"The man really was mafia, but he was low level. By the time they figured it out, they'd already paid me, and I'd already spent it. This whole thing could have been called off a year and a half ago, but the FBI doesn't like to admit when they're wrong. So, they decided to keep Marlena until his parole hearing came due. The fact that he got shanked was a fluke. We all got lucky. He was a horrible human being anyway, so I chalk his death up to karma. He killed someone years ago, and now someone killed him. End of story," Jeff says.

"Except that it's not," Susan argues. She's almost yellin'. "There's a guy out there who thinks someone's going to kill his family, so who knows what he's going to do. There's Meagan who has been missing her mother all this time, because she thought she was dead. And then there's you blaming Meagan for every problem between you and Mom when she's here because you're so greedy. If you didn't love money so much, we wouldn't be in this mess." She wipes away another tear. "A lot of people are worried and scared because of what you did, and you don't even feel the least bit sorry."

I dial the number again. "This is the Sheriff again. I wanted to tell you there is no threat left. You may go back to your family."

Marlena's green eyes are lookin' at me, and it feels mighty good. "You gonna take me on a date any time soon, Sheriff?"

I can't believe she's bein' so bold in front of all these people.

"Maybe," I say.

She walks over to stand beside me before doing a spin turn. Her left hand is on my left shoulder. Her back is turned to everyone else. She stands on tiptoe. "I might just end up back in that bed of yours yet," she purrs. "I've always wanted to tangle with the law."

I'm so glad I'm wearin' a long shirt. I can't believe I underestimated her ability to make me feel as uncomfortable as possible. "You really know how to torture a guy," I manage. *I've got steam comin' out my ears.*

"I'd prefer neither of you do anything until you walk down the aisle," Preacher says from across the room.

I laugh out loud. I can't help it.

"Still tryin' to make her an honest woman, Preacher?" I tease.

He frowns. "She's my sister, and I'm a Preacher. I'm just doing my job."

Marlena threads her fingers through mine, squeezin'. "It's his job to protect me day or night, Preacher. He's doing his civic duty."

Her brother stares the two of us down. "I'm pretty sure he doesn't give that much personal attention to all civilians."

Meagan looks like someone hit her upside the head. "You're my uncle," she asks. I'm so glad for the interruption. I'm not even close to bein' ready to talkin' to Preacher about what I'll be doin' or not doin' with his sister behind closed doors.

Preacher nods his head. "I am, and I have a few brothers, too."

"Are they married or are you all priests?" Meagan asks

He laughs. "They're married. They have children."

She bounces on her heels and claps her hands. "I have cousins."

He nods once more. "You do."

18

DAY SEVEN

I can't believe Meagan is nervous about going to a family reunion, or that she's demanding I go with her. Since Conrad knows her cousins, he's coming too. Dad traded his beloved Cavalier in three days ago for a mid-sized SUV. Mom says he's trying to be more family oriented, but that hardly matters to me. It's a little too late for that. I haven't spoken to dad since the Sheriff left our house yesterday. I can't believe all the shit he pulled for a wad of cash. I can't believe all the lies he told just to get Meagan out of our house. I still don't know if he's going to be charged with anything. I guess we'll cross that bridge when we get there, as Conrad loves to say."Here, take my car. It has more space," Dad says as he holds out his keys.

"But I don't have money for gas," I protest.

He hands me a twenty. "This should get you there. Have a nice time with everyone."

This is so strange. I'm still standing here trying to decide what to do, when Meagan breezes by me, snagging my arm. "Come on, we gotta go get Conrad. I don't want to be late."

"It's a family reunion," I tell her as we walk outside. "You can't be late."

"First impressions are very important," she insists. I can't believe how light her voice is, or how there's no tension. There's no wondering what she's going to do once we are out of sight of my parents' house. I'm not sure what to make of the new Meagan, but it's nice to see her so happy.

I pull up to Co's. She lays on the horn. I give her a shove. He jogs down the sidewalk. His eyes light up when he spies me sitting behind the wheel. "No way," he says.

I shrug and try to act all cool. "Dad said I could. It's just six blocks. Surely I can avoid the cops for that long."

He opens the back door. "This is so cool. My girlfriend drives a Subaru."

I can't help but giggle. "Dude. It's a station wagon."

Co sits in the middle of the backseat. He winks at me in the rearview mirror. "It's four wheel drive and all-terrain. It'll go anywhere," he says with a sense of wonder that makes him sound like a commercial.

Meagan grabs the side of her seat and turns back to look at him. "Yeah, it'll go anywhere, and we're going to *my* family reunion. How cool is that?"

I feel bad, but I feel like I should warn her. "You know how your grandma got pregnant, right?"

Co almost chokes. Meagan whips back around. "Yeah, but creepy sex offender grandpa is dead, so, he won't be there," she pops off.

I don't know what to say now, so I focus on the road ahead of me in between stealing glances thirty times in a minute at my speedometer. I am not getting a speeding ticket. "Well, that's good to know," Co answers, breaking the awkward silence.

"Do you think your mom likes the Sheriff?" I ask her, because I'm curious, but also I feel bad about what I just said.

"Stranger things have happened," she muses, and I can't disagree.

"Which cousin you gonna torment first," Co jokes.

"Whichever one gives me shit," Meagan replies, and I giggle some more. She's still feisty Meagan Davis to me, my best friend.

"I can't believe you're meeting everyone and then you're moving away," I say as we climb out of the car. I can smell the barbecue grill from here.

171

Meagan takes me my hand. Co takes my other. "Let's just enjoy today, shall we," Co says in his grown-up way that I love so much.

"Yes, we shall," Meagan replies as we head across the lawn.

19

SNACK TIME - LOADED BAKED POTATO

or once, I'm happy to take Kerin's words of advice, and they might be my favorite ones. She said any time I want to visit with Meagan, I should write her a letter and stick it in a box. So far as I know, Kerin knows as little as possible about the whole situation, but like many adults in my life, I think she knows more than she lets on, and I'm choosing to be okay with that. If there's anything I've learned since I thought I was an *accessory to murder*, it's that sometimes popping your own security bubble is necessary for survival.

"I hope it's safe to say the most thrilling chapter of your life is over and done with," Kerin says near the end of a quieter than usual forty-five minutes.

"Yeah," I say with a sigh. "I hope so, too."

"Catch me up on yearbook and forensics," she suggests, and I can't help but smile. Whether or not she meant to reference my code word for whatever me and Co are, I don't know, but I know the answer, and it's one I like way too much.

"It's going really good," I answer with a cheesy smile as I stand in her doorway. "See you next week?"

She taps her pencil on her desk with a smile. "See you next week."

Mom drives me home in silence. No radio. Something's bugging her. I hope it's not Co's and my daily study sessions. We hang out in my room with the door open. Always. We're G-rated. But I don't mind. There's a lot to be said for parental supervision, especially since I'm dating a guy that drives me crazy. I need as much of it as I can get.

Mom clears her throat as we pull into the driveway. "I left something on your bed." Her mysterious tone has my heart racing. It's from Meagan. I just know it. I was beginning to think she'd forgotten me altogether. I'm in the house and up the stairs. I fling my room door open, half expecting to see her standing there.

A small white envelope lays in the middle of my pale pink comforter covered with white clouds. I close the door behind me, snatch up the envelope, and flop back on my back before ripping it open.

Dear Susan,

I'm sorry that I could not be more of the friend you needed me to be, just like I'm sorry I must have been a terrible friend for you to think these last seven days have been another game of Crack-It. When I thought J remembered me, that he had come back for just me, I lost it. I guess I needed to know that someone was looking for me, even if it wasn't who I wanted it to be.

There's so much more I'd like to say about everything, but the less you know the better. I hope you can trust me when I say I withheld information to try to protect you. And I hope you can trust me when I say, as crappy of a friend as I have been, I'm really trying to change. If nothing else, your friendship has shown me that not everyone is a liar. Not everyone is out here to hurt me. I have to believe that. My family who I'm getting to know show me over and over I can trust people, especially my uncle, the Preacher.

But enough about me. What I want to say, is that I am choosing to hold onto the best parts of our friendship, and I hope you will to. Like the time we stayed up all night and ate so many jellybeans we both wanted to puke, or the time we spent the whole weekend stalking our crushes online like a couple of weirdos. Or the time we went with your parents to watch the Christmas tree lighting on the square, and after, we walked around sipping hot cocoa.

Or the time your mom took us to watch the city boys' choir at the church concert and their voices were so beautiful I cried. I'm sorry I lied to you about it and said I had allergies. I was so embarrassed. I couldn't believe I was crying over a bunch of twelve-year-old boys singing church songs, or that you promised me you would get me an allergy pill when we got home when I knew that you knew I didn't need one.

I hope you can hold onto all the good memories we had together too, and not just the bad ones. Even though I didn't show it very good, you made me want to be a better person, and I'm going to keep trying to be the person you think I can be instead of the angry girl I've been for so long.

I'm happy to be with my mom again, but I'll miss you, Susan. So much. You're the first real friend I ever had, and I hope I didn't ruin your faith in me. I'm working on forgiving my mom for leaving me behind even though it's hard. I'm working on that because I know you would tell me to.

Thank you, Susan, for sticking with me through all the good and the bad, like only a true friend would. I owe you more than I can ever repay, but if I know you, you're reading this and telling me I owe you nothing, because that's what friends are for. We stick together through thick and thin, even if it means being an Accessory to Meagan.

Her last line takes me by surprise, and I laugh through my tears. Only Meagan would say something like that or use her name as a synonym for murder. I fold her letter up and stick it back in the envelope, which I then slip into the back of my diary.

Dear Meagan,

This may be my first and last letter to you, I just don't know. It was so nice to hear from you one more time. There was so much left unsaid between us, and I didn't know it until I read your words. Just like always, you're one step ahead of me, but that's okay. Kerin says I should write to you to work through things, and so here goes:

I'm mad at you. I'm mad at you for leaving me in the dark for so long. I'm mad at you for letting me think I could hurt you as much as I did. I'm mad at you for all the games you played, and how you tried to rip me to pieces emotionally. And even though I know you were hurting, I'm still mad. But at least I have Kerin. You had no one. You could have used a Kerin. I hope you get to see someone you can talk to. I hope the chaos is behind you. I hope you let it all go and try to live a normal life. That's what I'm going to do.

I'm still dating Co. I think you approved. He's sweet, funny, and adorable, a word I try to remember not to call him, because he hates it, which makes him all the more adorable to me. I think he'd be happier to hear he's hot or drool-worthy, which he is in his own way but I'm not about to make that kind of confession, at least not to him.

I'm on yearbook and I'm in forensics. It turns out I have a real flare for drama and displays of great emotion. I guess all this trauma has its benefits.

It's going to take a lot of therapy to work through this past week. I wish I could be as blasé as you about being an Accessory to Meagan or Murder for seven days, take your pick, but I'm just not there yet. But there's one thing I know, as crazy as our friendship was, and as many shared crappy moments we had that I wish I could forget, there are just as many great ones I can hold onto, and that's what I'm going to do.

I'm sure I'll have many friends, but you'll always be my first best friend, and my first PIC.

Meagan + Susan = Crack-It forever.

THANK YOU FOR READING

––––––

Did you enjoy this book?

We invite you to leave a review at your favorite book site, such as Goodreads, Amazon, Barnes & Noble, etc.

DID YOU KNOW THAT LEAVING A REVIEW...

- Helps other readers find books they may enjoy.
- Gives you a chance to let your voice be heard.
- Gives authors recognition for their hard work.
- Doesn't have to be long. A sentence or two about why you liked the book will do.

ABOUT THE AUTHOR

I live in the beautiful Flint Hills of Kansas. I'm blessed to do two things I love- nursing and writing. I have wonderful family support including my husband, our son, daughter-in-law, and two daughters, my parents and in-laws, and too many more to mention as well as many friends who willingly give their input whenever it is requested. I'm thankful for the characters and stories as they come along, as well as the companies who publish them and readers who read them.

facebook.com/RachelAnneJonesAuthor

x.com/Jones1974Ra

instagram.com/diari197

tiktok.com/@idreamofdandelions

ALSO BY RACHEL ANNE JONES

With Satin Romance

A Joy-Filled Christmas

Fill Your Cup, Valentine

Pickles-N-Fries and Fireflies

Stealing the Glass Slipper

A Stolen Heart

Agent of Salt

The Last Living Beauty Queen

In Fields Where Love Grows

With Fire & Ice YA Books

Novels

Marmalade Uncapped

Essence of Emma

Lovestruck: Kisses, Lies & Oatmeal Cream Pies

Ramblin' Nash: A Day in the Life of a Flower Shop Boy

All Or Nothing Series

Chasing Denver

Rough Terrain

A Firm Plateau

Radioactive Series

Love and Armageddon

House of Cinders

M.I.A.

The X-Factor